STRUNG OUT

GIGI ARNOLD

DEDICATION

This book is dedicated to my mother who was my best friend and staunchest cheerleader. Although she is no longer with me, I know she is "working the room" wherever she is to help make my book a success.

ACKNOWLEDGMENTS

A big thank you to my husband, Steve, whose endless encouragement, editing and internet skills helped make this book possible. To my incredible sons, Dylan and Griffin, who inspire me daily. To Rob Lang of Redstart Graphics, my talented illustrator. To Mitch Smith, who helped format the cover for print. To Carlos A. Martir, Jr., criminal defense attorney extraordinaire, who educated me and helped me navigate the seamy world of murder and divorce. To Marsha Parish, retired FBI agent/tennis fanatic, who fascinated me with her undercover adventures and enlightened me with covert protocol; and finally, to my special and closest friends, Liz Siegel, Carrie Drazin, and Amy Mason who have always championed my writing and who really "get" me…I feel blessed to have you in my life.

CHAPTER 1

As I inched across a narrow bridge on the way to my first USTA tennis match, I did a double take as I passed a frowning clown driving in the opposite direction. I think I need to mention straight out that I have coulrophobia...a fear of clowns. He's just a guy in make-up, I kept repeating to myself. He's probably not going to kill you. He's just on his way to work. Work? It was 8:30 in the morning. What kind of work would a clown be doing this early? I immediately became suspicious. The clown was in full clown regalia: wild red hair, bulbous, red nose, painted red lips and polka-dotted clown suit. I was petrified.

It was a sign. I should never have played USTA this year. My life was already too stressful. I was in the middle of a nasty custody battle with my ex, my imbalanced editor at the Bucks Bugle told me I had to double as an investigative reporter (I was a food critic), and the most stressful of all: I was on a "power USTA team." My team, "High Strung", was serious about making it to districts. The team was mostly comprised of first and second court players who always won. Any loss on this team would be glaring.

Hello, my name is Charlotte McGhie. I kept my maiden name, thank you very much. I'm a divorced, 5' 5", 40-something, with shoulder length, dark brown hair, green eyes, and fair skin with way too many freckles. I'm half Irish, half Jewish, which equals a whole lot of neurosis and guilt.

As I carefully made my way off the bridge, I had a flashback to my first team meeting:

"I'm handing out a purple folder to everyone. Inside you'll find our team contact sheet, our schedule and a small piece of blank paper. I want you to write who you would like to play with and who you don't want to play with...although I'm not promising I can honor all of your requests," Elaine warned.

Elaine Cromwell was our 4.0 USTA captain. She was holding our first meeting at her house. Elaine was bossy and liked to be in charge a bit too much. She had wild, curly hair that was pulled back in a bushy ponytail. A few curls managed to escape, and she kept pushing them off her face.

I took a look around the room. My "don't play with" column quickly out-numbered my "play with" column. Everyone began buzzing about who was going to play with whom. There was whispering, clandestine meetings in corners, pencil tapping, biting, sighing and eye-rolling. In my "play with" column, I wrote down Jen Willow and "the new girl from Atlanta." I never saw her play and I didn't know her name, but she was from Georgia and she was gay and that's all I needed to know.

I folded my paper and handed it to Elaine. Elaine took a quick look and gave me a disapproving headshake. Elaine was nice enough, but she spoke in an annoying whine.

"Your 'play with' column only has two people in it," Elaine frowned.

"I know," I said.

"Well, I'm going to need you to be more flexible," Elaine said forcefully.

"I'll think about it," I said.

Jen took my arm and we went to get a glass of wine.

"I need a Valium," Jen said.

"I know," I agreed.

We glanced at Barb Calhoun. Her husband was a researcher at Tower-Glenn Pharmaceuticals. Barb was the team dealer. She always carried samples of everything.

"Hey, Barb," we said in unison. "What are you carrying?"

Barb rummaged through her purse. "Vicadin, Valium, Xanax, Ducolax, Tylenol, Crestor, or… Efferevescent anyone?"

"Thank goodness, not yet," I said. "I'll take a Valium and a Tylenol."

"Make that two," Jen echoed.

"Gel Caps or capsules?" asked Barb.

"Gel Caps" we said in unison.

Barb smiled. For some reason, giving out drugs made her happy.

"This meeting is always so stressful." Jen quickly gulped her pills and wine. "I wonder who's on the Pharma team this year?" asked Jen.

The Pharma team ("The Mood Swings") was comprised mostly of wives whose husbands worked for pharmaceutical companies. The Pharmas were real competitors, but since their husbands were always getting relocated to various parts of the country, the team changed a lot. I called the Pharma wives, the capsule clique. Their friendliness was time-released and they were always being a pain about something.

Suddenly my cell phone rang. It was my edgy editor, Edith Martin. "Yes, Edith, I'm on it." I clicked off my cell and waved good-bye to Jen and Elaine.

In my car, I went over my assignment in my head…scream by scream, just the way Edith shouted it to me: "Interview the principal at Langhorne Elementary School! Find out how Bucky the hamster died from eating a peanut chew! Interview the kids! Bribe the little bastards if you have to!" Great, I was on peanut patrol. This assignment was no problem for a real investigative reporter. I, however, was an investigative fill-in. I was officially hired as the Bugle's food critic. Bradley was the paper's investigative reporter. However, poor Bradley was in a body cast. He got body slammed by Sonia, the lap dancer, while investigating a strip joint in Bristol. Sonia was dancing on his table, slipped on some spilled beer and fell on top of him. That's the body part. The slam part that put him in a cast came from her jealous Mafia boyfriend, Sammy "the Squeeze" Santucci, who happened to be checking up on her. Sammy didn't expect to find her on top of Bradley. He picked up Bradley and threw him clear across the room. Bradley slammed right into a dancer's pole.

I played the scene over and over in my head.

"Edith, I'm a reviewer not an investigator," I had said to her. The biggest mystery I ever had to solve was why my sons' underwear keeps shrinking when I'm washing them in cold water."

Edith was too cheap to hire a legitimate replacement, so she asked me...told me...that I would be doing double duty for a while. I made a mental note to pick up one of those long scratcher things with the hand at the end for Bradley. Oh, yes, I also needed a bag of candy for kid bribing. A bag of iPods would be too costly.

I headed out of bucolic Washington's Crossing and made my way to a seedy section of Bristol. There seemed to be gas stations, convenience stores and strip clubs on every corner. I pulled into a "Gas and Go" station, and grabbed a variety of candy at the cash register...a variety that I liked, of course. An old boyfriend from high school was pumping gas. He smiled at me. He still didn't have his upper set of teeth. He was the pitcher for my high school baseball team and had them knocked out during a playoff game. His nickname was Funky. And boy, did he look it, now.

"Hi Funky!" I called.

"Hi Charlie, how ya been?"

"Busy, very busy," I said.

"I heard you got a divorce," Funky said hopefully.

"Yes, but it's way too soon to date," I lied. No reason to hurt his feelings. I had been divorced for about two years now. I noticed a beat up old green Dodge Dart parked by the side of the building. It couldn't be the same green Dodge Dart he used to pick me up on dates. He noticed me looking.

"Fucking bomb!" he muttered.

Funny that's the same thing he used to call the car while we were dating.

"Can I fill up your car?' he asked.

"No," I said.

"Change your oil?" he asked.

"No," I said again.

"Need anything greased?" he asked as he rubbed his dirty cloth in a circular motion over my headlights.

I thought I was going to throw up.

"Nothing changed, greased or filled," I said as I fumbled for my keys.

Funky pinned me to the car. His breath smelled of beer and stale cigarettes. As he opened his mouth to kiss me, I kneed him in the groin.

"Ooof!" Funky yelled.

"See ya around, Joe!"

As he held his groin, Funky tried to smile. He liked that I used his real name.

Langhorne Elementary School was a dump. Their playground was crumbling concrete, their basketball nets were ripped to shreds and graffiti was scribbled all over the building. I walked to the office and introduced myself to the secretary.

"Hi, my name is Charlotte McGhie. I'm a reporter for the Bucks Bugle. I was wondering if I could get a quick interview with the child who fed the hamster the peanut chew."

Before the secretary could open her mouth, Principal Paul came barreling out of his office.

"No comment. We have no comment. I said everything I had to say to the police."

"Can I just get a few words from the child?" I asked.

"We still don't know who had original possession of the peanut chew," the principal hesitated. No one is owning up to it...because of Bucky's passing. But, the whole class is devastated and with the school psychologist right now. And that's all I'm going to say on the matter."

I looked at the secretary. She wanted to tell me something. I pulled two Hershey bars out of my bag.

"Would either of you like a Hershey Bar?"

The secretary looked at the Principal. He shook his head no. She was defiant. "I'll take one. Thanks." She gave him a look. "The peanut chews were triple traded for a bag of Fritos, a TastyKake, and a Ring Ding."

"Anyone could have brought the peanut chews to school, found it in class or on school grounds," I said. Damn, I was good.

"No comment," the principal said again. "All I can say is that Langhorne Elementary is a peanut-free school."

"Thank you for your time," NOT, I thought.

I dejectedly walked out into the parking lot and got into my car. As I started the ignition, there was a tapping on my window. It was the secretary. I put down my window.

"I thought you should know that they're going to do an autopsy of Bucky."

"Who's 'they'?" I asked.

"Bucks County Animal Hospital in Warminster," the secretary whispered.

"Who did Bucky belong to?" I asked.

"Bucky was mine," said the principal."

Principal Paul tapped the secretary on her shoulder. The secretary jumped.

"She was giving me directions to Beaver Creek Park. I'm late for a tennis match," I said. Lie, lie, lie. Principal Paul already had his back turned. He was guiding the secretary into the school.

I shook my head as I drove over the bridge. Back to reality. Now was no time for flashbacks about work assignments. I needed to be alert and in the present. I needed to calm my nerves and pump myself up for my first USTA match. My team, "High Strung" was playing "The Mood Swings." I put in my Turtles CD. This was my "pump-up" music. Pathetic…right? My kids thought so. But, as I sang "You Baby" as loud as I could, it really relaxed me.

CHAPTER 2

As I pulled into the tennis club's parking lot, large raindrops started to pound against my windshield. I saw a crack of lightning streak across the sky. Heat lightning, I thought. Our match would be inside for sure.

Of all days to "be lunch." I lifted the huge crockpot from the trunk of my red RAV4 SUV and slung my tennis bag and other various bags of food items over my arms. I couldn't help but take note of all the BMW SUV's, Lexus SUV's, and various foreign sports cars in the parking lot. It did seem like most of the ladies I played tennis with owned luxury car companies, championship horses, or their husbands were Execs in pharmaceutical companies. And they were always complaining about how their CEO husbands were going to be let go because of downsizing. And, if that happened, what were they going to do without their yearly bonuses? As a single mom with a cheap ex-husband and a low-paying stressful job, I had little sympathy for these women.

"Hey Charlie, do you need some help?" Barb asked

"Thanks, Barb. Can you carry the crockpot? It's empty, so it's not heavy."

"No, problem," said Barb. "I'm glad we're inside today. Much rather play indoors."

We glanced quickly at an exterminating truck parked in the lot. There was a picture of a large cockroach painted on the side with a slash mark running through it. We gave each other a "yucky" face. Memo to self to make sure the lid is kept tight on the soup.

We ran inside as fast as we could. As I set everything up on the table in the lobby, I noticed Elaine was in a frenzy. "What's up?" I asked Maryellen, a fellow teammate.

"Elaine can't find her clipboard, and she's accused the other captain of stealing it. Now they're going to know our line-up and then they'll change their line-up."

"If they stole it," I said.

"Grace's team really wants to go to Districts. I think we have the same win/loss record. I wouldn't put it past them to steal it," Maryellen said.

"Found it!" I heard Elaine scream.

"Where was it?" Maryellen asked.

"On the floor behind the water cooler," Elaine said. She was glaring at Grace.

Grace was big and intimidating. She walked straight up to Elaine. "Are you accusing me of stealing your line-up?"

"I, I might," Elaine said.

"I don't like being accused. You got that?"

Oh, lord, are we going to have a rumble now? Yeah, let's take our tennis racquets out to the parking lot. The women with those gigantic oversized racquets, with the huge sweet spots will clearly have an advantage. Can you picture 16 perimenopausal women in the parking lot swinging racquets at each other? The sad truth was, yes, I could picture it and it almost happened two summers ago. Although, racquet sizes were smaller then and maybe things wouldn't have gotten so bloody. One girl accused her opponent of cheating all through the match. So, she decided she was going to call a ball out that was really good to teach her a lesson. One thing led to another and the cheater told the cheat-ee that she wanted to "take her out to the parking lot."

Back to today's match. Where was this famous line-up? I wanted to take a look to make sure I was playing with Jen. I looked at Jen. She was trying to steady herself against a couch. She seemed a little wobbly to me. Jen was an awesome tennis player, but she had a nasty habit of drinking before …okay, and after matches. She said it calmed her down. I think she was an alcoholic.

I smelled her breath. It smelled like 100 proof crème de menthe.

"I stopped at Jitters and got a coffee, " Jen said defensively.

Jitters was a high-end coffee shop that was always buzzing with people.

"Jitters doesn't sell alcohol," I said. I unzipped the little pocket of her tennis bag and pulled out a cute bottle of crème de menthe. It was empty.

"Jen!"

"It was a souvenir from our Jamaican flight. Party, party, party," hiccupped, Jen.

Elaine began to shout. "Ladies, it's raining outside so we're playing indoors. Use the 10-point Komen tiebreak for the 3rd set. Your court numbers are on your can of balls at the desk. Good luck and just have fun!"

"Yeah, right," I said to Jen. "'Just have fun', but you know and I know that Elaine is not going to play us a lot if we lose."

"Elaine's annoying but I don't think she would do that," Jen said.

As we walked onto the court, I was steadying Jen from behind. Then Grace walked on with her partner Lilly. They were wearing matching yellow outfits. Grace was about 5' 10" and really big. Lilly was short and stout. She was known in tennis circles as "plug" because she was built like a fire hydrant. Plus, she was curiously missing a neck. It was like her head went right into her body. Grace and Plug were both wearing matching visors. Don't get me started about women who wear visors indoors. What is that about?

The warm-up was really annoying. "She's trying to win the warm-up", I said to Jen. "Grace keeps hitting searing winners up the alley. I don't think she's hit me one forehand yet."

"I hate that," said Jen. "Well, at least she's hitting it back to you. Plug keeps hitting everything long or in the net. Let's go up."

We both started volleying and again Grace was just beaming balls up the alley or out of my reach crosscourt. Plug was either hitting the balls in the net or over Jen's head. This was clear gamesmanship. They obviously didn't want us to have a good warm-up.

"Let's warm each other up," I said to Jen.

"Grace is going to have bird," Jen hiccupped.

Jen walked over to the other side.

"We're warming each other up," I said to Grace and Plug. "Neither one of you has hit us a decent ball."

"You can't do that," screamed Grace.

"It's in The Code. You're not hitting to us, so we're allowed to warm each other up." The Code, was the bible for tennis protocol when there wasn't an umpire or tennis official.

The warm up was finally over and the four of us approached the net.

"Up or down," I said, spinning my racquet.

"Up," Grace said.

"Down," I said.

Although Jen and I warmed each other up, it didn't help. We lost the first set 6-4. As Jen and I switched sides, we smelled something terrible wafting from the walls.

"It smells like something died in there," said Jen. "A dead animal?"

I took a whiff. "Cheaters from USTA past." Ladies tennis eats its own.

"Any thoughts?" Jen asked.

"Well, how about I play ad and you play deuce," I suggested.

It didn't help.

It was 5-6, 2nd set, and my turn to serve. I served what I clearly thought was an ace.

"Back!" Grace yelled.

"By how much?" Jen asked.

"Enough that it was back," Grace said.

My hands were shaking. I double-faulted my second serve, which I almost never did. We battled the next few points, until it was deuce. I hit another beautiful serve.

"Foot fault," I heard across the court.

"Excuse me?" I asked incredulously.

"It's our point. You had a foot fault," Grace yelled louder.

Jen looked at me, wondering which way we were going on this. I went with indignant.

"All of a sudden you decide to call a foot fault the first time in the match?" I shouted. "You need to give me a warning first. It's in 'The Code.'"

"Again with The Code. You've been foot faulting the whole time and this is a crucial point," Grace groused.

Women are such bitches, I thought. And USTA brought out the worst in them.

"Ad out", I moaned. As I began my service motion, instead of thinking about where I wanted to place my serve, I was thinking about keeping my left foot still. I chased a bad toss.

"Foot fault!" Grace and Plug screamed in unison.

I was fuming. I hate them. I hate USTA. I hate playing on a court that smelled like dead bodies. Jen walked back to the base line and gave me what I thought would be a little pep talk.

"Shake if off and hit the crap out of that ball. You should feel blessed that you're able to play tennis at your age." Jen hiccupped again.

"My age? Thanks a lot, Jen! Is this your idea of a pep talk? I don't think I'm ready for Tai Chi in the park yet!" I was 44, but most people thought I looked like I was in my early 30's. I chalked it up to the Irish part of my heritage. We were a youthful people. I had classic Black Irish coloring: Dark hair, green eyes, light skin and freckles. My mind started to wander to the movie, "Finnegan's Rainbow." I grew up believing in leprechauns and sappy musicals. I shook my head. I needed to concentrate on my second serve. If I lost it, Grumpy and Dumpy would win the match.

I started my service motion and Grace started stamping her feet. I stopped.

"You can't do that," I shouted.

"I can do whatever I want to do," Grace retorted.

"Stamping your feet during my service motion is a hindrance," I said. "It's in the Code. Item 34."

"Every time you have a problem with something, you say it's in the Code. You're lying!" said Plug.

"I have a copy in my bag," I said. "I'll show you." And, it's because of jerks like you that I carry a copy with me.

"You're bluffing. Just serve!" Grace gave a heavy sigh.

I looked at Grace, ready to receive. She was loudly stamping her feet. I looked at Grace's team, cheering them on from the window. I looked at their team co-captain. She was giving Grace and Lilly, elaborate baseball-like hand signals. Tai Chi was looking pretty darn good at this point.

I took a deep breath and exhaled. "Second serve," I called out. I spun my second serve deep into the box, but Grace hit it for a winner down the line. Cheers exploded from the window. I felt a tear making its way down my cheek. Jen hugged me.

"Not bad, for an old bitch!" said Jen. We both laughed.

I quickly left the court to make my salad and get the soup ready. I poured the soup I had made into the crockpot. After my humiliating defeat, I had the pleasure of serving Grace and her fellow cretins a gourmet lunch. I had made chicken tortilla soup and a mixed green salad with goat cheese, cranberries and caramelized walnuts. Dessert was strawberry shortcake. As was customary, our team let the other team serve themselves first. Grace and Plug, were first in line. Plug accidentally bumped the bowls off the serving table. Actually, Plug's big butt knocked over the bowls. While she was grabbing utensils, her butt was busy elsewhere. Plug turned around to pick up the bowls, but her butt backed into the ice bucket, causing the cubes to scatter on the floor. While my team and I were picking up ice, Grace continued to chow down on the soup. She even took a second helping before anyone else got firsts.

Suddenly we were picking something else off the floor. It was Grace. She keeled over, taking the crockpot with her.

Chicken tortilla soup splashed all over our matching turquoise outfits.

"I think Grace had a heart attack, " I heard someone yell. "Someone give her mouth-to-mouth," another called out.

We all looked at each other. No one was stepping forward to suck face with Grace.

"I'm giving her the Heimlich maneuver said Plug." Plug tried with all her might to squeeze Grace from behind, but she just couldn't do it. She laid Grace back down.

Maria Theresa stood over Grace and crossed herself. Maria Theresa was the team Pope for the Mood Swings. She was rubbing her over-sized cross necklace as she glared at me. It was the "biggie-fries" of crosses. You heard of people wearing their heart on their sleeve, well, Maria Theresa wore her cross on her chest like a movie billboard. Only, Maria's boobs were a coming attraction no one wanted to see. Maria Theresa was a seasoned tennis player. She knew what she was doing with that cross. She was big, blonde and bodacious. The cross dangled strategically at the top of her enormous cleavage, for all the world…and her tennis opponents to see. No one dare question Maria Theresa about a line call. The Pope wouldn't lie. During a fast-paced volley exchange at the net, sometimes it would be hard to concentrate on the ball. Your eye would naturally gravitate to Maria Theresa's cross swinging back and forth, back and forth just grazing the tops of her breasts. It was as if she was trying to hypnotize her opponents…or make them turn gay, or, better yet…Catholic. Her current husband, Dal, a retired monk, was standing next to her. He came to most of her matches still dressed in "uniform". We all swore that the reason Maria Theresa won so much was because Dal possessed some secret Divine magic powers. But, what could we do? It would be like accusing Gandhi.

Maria Theresa shook her head. "This might be God's will, but it's definitely gonna screw up our line-up for next week. Grace was supposed to play singles and we don't have another singles player."

I looked at Grace. Her head was lying in a pool of soup. Her mouth open, as if ready to receive another spoonful….or Eucharist from Maria Theresa.

I felt horrible that Grace and I had argued on the court. As I went to move her head, Elaine yelled at me. "Don't move her! That could make it worse. Don't you watch House?"

I ignored her and felt Grace's pulse. "She's dead!" I gently dropped her wrist.

There was a moment of stunned silence in the room, and then activity resumed again.

Cindee Squire, the club manager called 911 on her cell. Actually, we were all on our cells. We were calling husbands, sitters, girlfriends, hairdressers….this was prime gossip. We soon heard the emergency sirens and a stretcher was brought in. Police started casing the joint. We were all told not to leave the building.

My teammates immediately took action:

"Are there any drills?" Melanie inquired at the front desk. A few other girls joined her. If they couldn't leave the building, they might as well play tennis. There were 6 indoor courts at the Mill Creek Tennis Club.

"Is, uh, Chad, available?" asked Kathy. "For a private?" Chad was the hot new tennis pro from LA.

The sharp bark of a cop brought me back to reality.

"I understand you made the soup," said the cop.

"Yes, that's true," I said hesitantly. Was I incriminating myself? Did I have the right to ask for a lawyer before I answered any more questions? My mind became a Rolodex of crime shows, flipping through different episodes, looking for the ones that had anything to do with tortilla soup and dead, obnoxious, tennis players.

"We're taking the soup back to the lab," snapped the cop.

"Not to eat I hope," I smiled. I was looking for the cop's nametag hoping if I personalized the conversation, he would be nicer to me.

The cop just gave me a blank look.

Yeesh, this cop had no sense of humor. I wanted a Chris Noth cop. Actually, I didn't know if Chris Noth had a sense of humor. I just knew I wanted Chris Noth.

"This is serious, Miss…." Now the cop seemed to be looking for my nametag.

"Charlotte McGhie. But, you can call me Charlie." This didn't win him over, either.

"Well, Charlie, here's my card. Don't leave town," barked the cop again.

"You don't think I killed her, do you?" I asked incredulously. This cop was a nut. I was a member of Green Peace for goodness sake. I didn't eat red meat, only ate fish that weren't on the endangered species list, and I recycled everything…even old boyfriends. I was always giving them second chances.

"We're not calling this a murder…yet. You're just a person of interest," said the cop.

"You like brunettes, huh?" I batted my green eyes at him. No reaction. This cop must have decided long ago that having a personality was a job negative.

I glanced at the card he had given me. His name was Tevya . As in, "Fiddler on the Roof", "Tevya." I started laughing out loud.

"Something funny?" Tevya asked.

"Did you ever see 'Fiddler On The Roof?' He just stared at me. "You know, Tevya from 'Fidler on the Roof.' 'Tradition, tradition,'" I sang. I started to really get into the song with both hands up in the air, pivoting in a circle and dovening up and down…just like the production number. '….Tradition, tradition."

He gave me a look somewhere between horror and disgust, like I just passed gas.

"My whole name couldn't fit on the name tag. It's Tevyalexski. I'm Polish. You have a problem with that?

He glared at me. Well, he certainly had the staring and glaring thing down.

"My friends call me Alex. But, only my friends."

And with that, the cop walked away and conferred with the other cops who had been questioning the various players in the club.

I glanced over at the other team. They were huddled in cliques.

I saw two pros staring at me, Eddie and Luke. Eddie said something to Luke and they laughed. Then Luke handed Eddie some bills. Eddie was always betting on something. I guess he was betting that I was guilty.

I saw Chad and his flock head to court 1. Did he have disability insurance, I wondered? I wouldn't be surprised if he slipped on all the drool dripping from their mouths. I saw Eddie giving Chad a dirty look as he walked up to the desk.

The cops had put on plastic gloves and were now scouring the carpet, trying to mop up soup samples, I guessed. They were putting small samples of carpet in tiny envelopes. They huddled and looked over at me. What's with all the huddling?

I waved and then went downstairs to the lower level to drop off my racquet. It needed to be restrung. Henry, the stringer, gave me a funny look. Well, that's all right, because he gave me the creeps.

"Hi Henry," I said. Henry just nodded. "Uh, I'm looking for a little more feel when I hit, can you give me 17 gauge this time and string it a little looser, maybe 55 pounds?" Henry nodded. "Can I pick it up before the weekend?"

"You think you're going to be playing over the weekend?" Henry seemed skeptical.

"Why wouldn't I be playing? Do you know something I don't know?"

"Are you a religious woman, Charlotte?" asked Henry.

"No, not really," I said.

"I didn't think so," scoffed Henry. "A religious woman would be spending the weekend praying for forgiveness, not running around on a tennis court."

I grabbed my racquet back from him. "The last time I looked at the constitution, people were innocent till proven guilty."

Henry pulled a jack knife out of his pocket. He started sawing a string in half. He held the knife up to me. "Thou shalt not kill."

"I didn't kill anyone!"

I looked around. Where were all the people? I was alone with this nut. Suddenly, Cindee popped her head in the room.

"Charlie, we need you upstairs. Hi Henry. When do you think you'll be finished stringing Geri Vale's racquet?"

Henry's whole demeanor changed. "I should be finished in 10 minutes, Miss Squires. I changed her grip for her, too. It looked a little ratty."

"You're the best, Henry!" smiled Cindee. Cindee scooted upstairs.

Henry gave me an evil grin as he knotted a string and pulled it taut.

When I walked upstairs, both teams were sitting opposite each other on couches. Everyone's racquets and bags had been thrown into a pile in the center of the floor. I added my racquet to the pile. About a half dozen cops, all wearing plastic gloves were rifling through the bags. The cops already had my bag. All eyes were on me....with Maria Theresa contributing an extra set....her evil eye. I stared at her. I mouthed, "I'm innocent." Maria Theresa glared at me and crossed herself.

I took note of the rest of the team, wondering if any of them could have done it. There was Collette Cousteau... great granddaughter of Jacques. Collette, although having lived in the states for 20 years, still had a thick, French accent. She was a chain-smoker, who always looked nervous when she didn't have a cigarette in her hand. She had a Pucci scarf, knotted just so, around her neck, that she was playing with. Her husband was a bigwig with Tower Glenn in France until they got relocated here. She was whispering to Jazzy Kincaid. Jazzy, real name, Jerry-Lee, never met a piece of gossip she didn't want to repeat. She and Collette kept glancing at me. I smiled and waved. Jazzy gave me the finger. How sweet. Plug, still in shock over Grace, was crying uncontrollably into her Kleenex. So was Andi, Tammy,

Ginger and Jessie. Actually, all three were crying in between their texting.

I nervously took a seat next to some of my teammates: Jen, Barb, Devon. Susie and Maryellen. Devon didn't look happy. "Nice going, Charlie. If our team gets DQ'd for Districts because you murdered Grace, you're off the team."

"Who made you captain?" I asked. The question was rhetorical. Nobody made Devon captain. She was one of our valued singles players and one of the strongest women on the team. So, Devon could do and say anything she wanted. She was ruthless and was serious about the team going all the way to Nationals.

An oversized cop, chomping on what seemed like a whole pack of gum, furrowed his brow, trying to silently stare us down. Finally, he spoke.

"Y'all got anything to say? This here's a serious situation that could land someone in jail for a long, long time."

I whispered to Jen. "A Southern cop, we're in trouble. Did you ever see the movie, "In the Heat of the Night, with Sidney…"

"You got somethin' to say, Missy?" The oversized cop was looking at me. "Why don't you share what you were sayin' with all of us."

"I, I was just asking my friend if she ever saw the movie, 'In the Heat of the Night,' because you remind me of the police chief in that movie."

"In the heat of the what?" Oversized asked.

"'The Night.' You know, fish-out-of-water, Philadelphia cop, finds himself in competition with a Southern cop…"

No reaction from anyone in the room.

"I guess I'm dating myself. (beat) Which is a good thing, because no one else is!" I tapped the table with a badump bump. Yessiree, resort to bad stand-up comedy routine when face-to-face with humorless cop who wants to put you behind bars.

Suddenly, Mr. Oversize's demeanor changed. "Really? Ah look like a movie actah? What's his name?"

"Rod Steiger. And, he also won for best actor that year, 1967." I was hoping I sounded enough like Roger Ebert to be ruled out as a murder suspect. I mean, who would suspect an elite film critic of committing murder.

"Well, now, Missy. This ain't no movie. And, ah believe it was you who made the soup that could have killed everyone in this room."

"With all due respect, Mr. Oversize…" Shit! Did I just call him that?

Maria Theresa crossed herself again. My teammates were cringing. They covered their faces with their hands.

I had a vision of me in striped, jail pajamas pleading in front of the judge. "Please have mercy on me, judge. I have a history of blurting out inappropriate things. I can't help it." The judge doesn't care. "You are now sentenced to life in prison for saying too many stupid things, too many times."

I tried to regain my composure. Unfortunately, along with my blurting out inappropriate things way too often, I also had a bad habit of challenging authority figures that dated back to getting kicked out of the Brownies at 10 and overnight camp at 13.

I stood up. "On behalf of everyone here, we all plead the 5th, and refuse to say anything else until we have proper legal representation."

My teammates looked doubly petrified after I said this. I didn't care. I was Atticus Finch. I had smarts and integrity and would not be pushed around.

Jazzy raised her hand. "She doesn't represent our team! We have nothing to hide. We don't need the 5th." Jazzy's team all nodded in agreement.

Elaine raised her hand, too. "She doesn't represent me, or my team, either."

Traitors! All of them.

"What makes you so sure it was something in the soup that killed her? She could have had an allergic reaction to…to…tortillas, or…or chicken….or tomatoes, or cilantro, or…" What the heck else was in there? "Chicken broth." I tried to sound as convincing as I could.

Elaine rolled her eyes. "No one is allergic to chicken broth. Something poisonous must have been added to the soup to have killed her."

Everyone in the room let out a loud gasp. "Thanks, Elaine. Because I didn't win my match you're turning on me. What a great way to get me off your team. Indict me for murder." Why did I say the "M" word?

Everyone let out a loud gasp again.

"Maybe you put something in the soup, Elaine," said Jen.

"That's ludicrous," said Elaine.

Jen continued. "You asked to be on Grace's team two years ago and she said she'd pass.

"Well, now she did pass," Elaine said sarcastically.

"It makes more sense for Charlie to have killed her," Elaine said. "Charlie was on Grace's team last summer and she didn't play her in Districts…or Sectionals. I heard Charlie crying about it in the bathroom."

The two cops obviously were not used to tennis drama and had no idea what Elaine was talking about. Only serious tennis players understood the pride that was associated with having your captain trust you enough to play you in Districts and Sectionals. But, to kill someone over bruised pride?

Alex sighed and approached Elaine. "Are you seriously telling me that not playing someone in a tennis tournament is motive enough to kill them?

Elaine's face flushed. "Yes, yes I am. Because we're not talking about just any tennis tournament….we're talking Districts…and Sectionals! Charlie is a nice girl, but everyone knows she hasn't been emotionally stable for several years now. As far as I'm concerned, not being played last summer put her over the edge."

My mouth was agape like a guppy on steroids.

Maria Theresa nodded in agreement. "It's true. Lord knows, we all have our troubles (cross), but Charlie's been having a hard time coping with her divorce and keeping her job (cross). And, those kids of hers are really a handful (shake of head and cross)."

Mouth opened even wider now. "Maria Theresa, you never even met my kids."

"We've all heard how disrespectful they are. It's because they're left alone too much. You're juggling too many plates." (Looks over to where Grace collapsed) "And, now you see what can happen when you juggle too many plates. I think we need a moment of silence for Grace."

Her team agreed. They all closed their eyes and hung their heads. Academy Award anyone?

Alex tried to take control again. "You are all free to leave after you have filled out these forms with your names, phone numbers and email addresses. No one is to travel outside the state until further notification. Notifying a lawyer of today's events would not be a bad thing."

Mr. Oversized just scowled at me and whispered something to Alex. Henry walked into the room and whispered something to Oversized. What was that about? Oversized then whispered it to Alex. The HORSE whisperer, I thought….smiling at my own joke.

"Ms. McGhie," said Alex. "Can you empty out your handbag for us."

I emptied out my handbag. "See, no poison." Except for the three small vials of clear liquid that fell to the table, and rolled onto the floor. Everyone in the room gasped. "That's not mine. Someone put that in my purse."

"Ms. McGhie, I suggest you go home and find yourself a good lawyer," said Alex.

Driving home, I started to think about the implications of Grace's death. I probably would be charged with involuntary manslaughter…even though I didn't spike the soup. But, to prove that, I would need a hotshot lawyer, preferably one of those celebrity lawyers that were always popping up on the Larry King show. I think OJ's lawyer was dead. Rats! Doesn't matter, I'm not a celebrity…or rich. Who am I kidding? The only lawyer I could afford would have to work on school snack money. So, my kids wouldn't eat snack for a month. And, of course, I'd have to give up my weekly Mah Jongg game, even though we only played for quarters. Tennis drills were out, which meant I would get very heavy and cranky. Who would take care of my kids while I was in the slammer? My creepy ex-husband? Scenes of Dumbo crying while he looked through the prison bars at his mother flashed through my mind. I hit myself in the head. This was one random thought, too many.

Who the heck would kill Grace? Yes, she was annoying, and she did have a reputation for cheating on line calls, but that's no reason for killing her. Okay, and she did humiliate me by not playing me in Districts and Sectionals. But, whoever poisoned the soup had no idea Grace would be the one to eat it first. The whole team could have died. Someone was obviously trying to frame me, but why?

CHAPTER 3

Morning in the Green/Mcghie household was hectic, yet slow-paced. We were the oxymorons of households. There was a lot to do to get the kids ready for school, but none of us were morning people. We were in a perpetual state of slow motion, until I had my coffee, that is. School mornings were the only time I missed my ex, Marshall Green. Marshall was a morning person who ran a tighter ship than Captain Von Trapp. He would always let me sleep an extra half hour while he fed and organized our 10 year-old, Jake and our 14 year-old Josh.

I guess he was counting on me sleeping through his cheating, too. Poker night at his best friend Todd's, turned out to be "Poke Her" night. For this past year, there never was a Friday night game. I knew Marshall worked hard and never wanted to bother him over at Todd's. He needed the relaxation, I thought. But, one fateful Friday night, Jake was running a high fever and I needed to take him to emergency. I called over to Todd's to see if Marshall could come home and watch Josh. Todd, not being the greatest of liars, became flustered when I insisted on talking to Marshall. His weak "Marshall is in the bathroom," became, "Marshall is with Gayle an exotic dancer...I mean aerobics instructor, and they're at a cheap motel in Bensalem." Yep, Todd never could keep a secret.

Marshall led Gayle on, all year, promising to marry her. Well, that movie-of-the-week, actually had a happy ending…for her! They're married, and Gayle is pregnant. Ugh!

"Mom, Mom, did you sign this? And this?" Jake asked hurriedly.

"Your report card?"

"Interim," Jake corrected.

When did that come home?" I asked.

"Last week. I need to return it today, or else I'll get a detention."

"Mom, can you drive me to school?" asked Josh looking at the clock.

"Do you have snack money?" I asked him

"No."

"Do you have your soccer or basketball sneakers?" I wasn't sure which school sport Josh was doing now. And could he use his soccer shoes for track, if that happened to be the sport of the season.

"They're called, cleats, Mom. I have my cleats. I just need money for snack and a drink and I need you to pick me up at the high school today. We have a track meet. Oh, and I need money for a lunch ticket. And money for the school trip to Rip-Ride Park," Josh said, hurriedly.

I was gingerly emptying out our "vacation" jar money. Just pennies. Rats! I ran to get my Mah Jongg purse. Luckily, I had won quite a few hands this week.

"Mom, I'm gonna be late. Mom!" Josh was eyeing the clock again.

"I'm coming!" I yelled, running down the steps. My fists were full of quarters.

"Jakie, pour yourself some juice and eat a banana," I yelled, as Josh and I flew towards the door.

Suddenly, the phone rang.

"Don't get the phone unless you know who it is!" I yelled as I slammed the door shut.

When I returned 15 minutes later, Jake was sitting on the steps outside the house looking pale.

"Jake, what is it?" I asked, running up to him.

"Well, I picked up the phone by mistake." Jake said slowly.

"And, and…" I was worried now.

"It was a woman's voice. She said, 'Tell your mother that she would be the next one to die.'"

Jake started to cry. I cradled him in my arms.

"What an awful person," I said. "What a sick, awful, person."

We went back inside and I looked at the caller ID. The number did not look familiar.

I had to calm Jake.

"Jake, do you want to go to Mount Fuji for dinner?"

Jake's eyes lit up. He loved the hibachi table show. I actually needed to review the restaurant for my food column in the Bucks Bugle. My newspaper would pick up the tab. Man can't live by Mah Jongg quarters alone. I drove Jake to the bus stop and waited till he got on the bus.

Then I drove to my 9:00 am tennis match in Washington's Crossing. We were playing the "Leave it to Beavers" team at Beaver Creek Park.

Fifteen minutes later, I pulled into the lot of Beaver Creek. The park was gorgeous. There were tall lush trees, ornate fountains and tennis courts as far as the eye could see.

I was playing with Savannah Charles. The more I learned about her, the more she intrigued me. She was a debutante in her youth and had her coming out party two years ago (before she moved), but "came out" again, just last week, when she announced to the team that she was gay. The Atlanta transplant was a thin, tall, lefty who never met a ball she didn't want to poach. We had done really well together in practice matches.

Beaver Creek was one of the tougher teams and would be a good test of how well we meshed as partners. I saw Elaine. She waved me onto the court where Savannah was taking practice serves.

"Hi," I said to Elaine.

"Ha," said Savannah, walking off the court. She had a really thick Southern accent. "Lordy, just the name of this team really turns me on."

"What are you talking about?" I asked.

"Beavah Creek," said Savannah dreamily.

"I don't get it." But after a second, I did get it. Savannah was gay, and Beavers were, yeah. I lightly hit Savannah on the head with my tennis racquet.

"What was that for?" asked Savannah…startled.

"First we win, then you can check out all the Leave it to Beavers you want." I said. "We're playing the Barbie Dolls. Brenda is the brunette and Julie is the blonde. They're good, they're crafty and…"

Just then, the Barbie's walked onto the court.

"…and they both have implants…," said Savannah.

"Well, yes, they do both have breast implants."

Damn, they were wearing their trademark tight, matching, low-cut tops. I hit Savannah again on the head.

"What was that for? Is this a Northern thing?" Savannah was annoyed.

"No, this is a tennis thing. You need to get your mind out of their cleavage and into the match," I said. She was still fixated on their breasts. I snapped my fingers several times in front of her eyes. "Is this mating season for you?"

"Listen, honey, to play good tennis, ah need to be relaxed. Ah need to have fun. "What do you call an Alabama farmer with a sheep under each arm?"

"What?" I sighed.

"A pimp! See, we're havin' fun now! Now, let's kick ass!"

And, kick ass we did. We won the first set easily, 6-2. I don't think the Barbie's knew what hit them. We were up in the second set, 4-1, and I could have sworn that the Barbies started flirting with Savannah…to get her distracted. When either of them bent down to pick up a ball, they lingered way too long. Then they would huddle and giggle. I knew what they were up to….and so did Savannah. Luckily, this just made Savannah mad. Yes, she was gay, she was horny, and she liked beavers way too much, but she would not be made a fool of. We beat the Barbie's, 6-1 in the second set.

Captain Elaine was elated. "Way to go, guys! We won the match 3-2. Both our singles won and you won."

The home team set up lunch on a picnic table. I was ravenous. As I was about to bite into my sandwich, my cell phone rang. I looked at the number. It was imbecilic, Edith.

"Hello, Edith." I held the phone away from my ear. "Yep. I'm on my way to the meeting."

I said good-bye to Savannah, waved to Elaine, and quickly hopped into my Red RAV4.

Then, I drove to my "office" (a corner cubicle) at the Bucks Bugle. I was late to the staff meeting, as usual. I pushed through the double glass doors of the conference room. Luckily, there was a seat next to Robin, my best friend. Robin Goldberg worked in the travel section. Actually, Robin was the travel section, which at first glance, sounds glamorous. But, because the Bugle was downright cheap, travel could mean anything from a tubing trip down the Delaware River to a "Pocono's can be posh! Get-A-Way." Her current assignment was, "Doing Doylestown on a Dollar." Yep, stretching that buck was a constant Bugle theme.

"What did I miss?" I whispered to Robin.

"You!" Robin whispered back. "The Bugle has you on the front page tomorrow."

"Typical Bugle mentality," I whispered back. "Our country is on the verge of a nuclear showdown with North Korea, there's rampant starvation and government coups in the Congo, Global Warming has been called the culprit for the latest disaster hurricane in the Carolinas, and I'm on the front page because I made the chicken tortilla soup that Grace ate." I was beside myself.

"Charlie, Robin, if you girls can't be quiet, we're going to have to separate you," Edith our Edwardian editor chided.

Robin and I thought Edith must have channeled the 19th century for her personality. With her thinning, red hair, red lips and conservative buttoned-up blouses and Little House on the Prairie skirt s, Edith was a cross between Queen Elizabeth the

1st and Maggie Smith from The Prime of Miss Jean Brody. Edith was harsh.

"Sorry, Edith," I said.

"Who haven't we heard from?" Edith asked.

Stan, the Bugle's accountant raised his hand.

"You've got the floor, Stanley," Edith smiled.

Edith and Stanley were having an affair.

Robin whispered to me again. "Don't get mad at me. I'm just the messenger. Roscoe Minsk speculated that you killing Grace was payback for Grace not playing you in Districts last year. I do remember you telling me how humiliated you felt."

I glared at Roscoe sitting at the end of the large conference table. He was eating a messy jelly doughnut that had dribbled on his tie.

"Roscoe Minsk is a dolt!" I whispered back. Roscoe was content editor at the Bugle. Roscoe had asked me to go to the prom my senior year in high school, and I turned him down. Ever since, Roscoe was always looking for opportunities to bad-mouth me.

"Roscoe's the one preoccupied with payback," I said a little too loudly.

Suddenly, the whole room went quiet. Prudence Campbell, our weather expert, let out an inappropriate giggle, and then a sing-song, "I think a cold front's coming." Prudence had been writing the weather column way too long. She now spoke only in climate clichés.

"Charlie, can I see you in my office?" Edith asked sternly.

Roscoe gave me a smirk. I smirked right back at him and followed Edith down the hall toward the window-lined offices.

"Charlie, let me start off by saying, I like you. You're funny, bright, attractive...."

Attractive? Maybe Robin and I had Edith pegged all wrong. Maybe Edith wasn't as schoolmarmish as we thought. Maybe what she wanted was a threesome...her, Stan and me. Ugh!

"....and a darn good writer...," Edith and her lipstick were smiling. Then she stopped smiling. She put her laced boot up on the chair I was sitting on. "But, I won't have you putting the

Bugle in jeopardy. You hear me? If you've killed somebody, that's your business. But, the minute it affects Bugle sales, well, that's my business. And, I swear I'll put your bony butt behind bars if I find out you've done anything illegal." She began petting my hair. I shivered. Edith had morphed from Queen Elizabeth to Marlena Dietrich in a matter of minutes. All I could think about was getting out of Edith's office alive…and with my clothes on.

I stood up. "Edith, I swear I'm innocent. I was set up. But, I'm going to find out who killed Grace."

"You're damn right you're going to find out," screeched Edith. "This could be a big story for the Bugle. I want the inside scoop. You know that Bradley is still in the hospital…" Edith's shouting continued to pound my head. "So, I'm going to need you to fill Bradley's shoes for awhile," said Edith

Well, that wouldn't be too much of a problem, I thought. Bradley was a "dwarf." I could fill Bradley's shoes several times over and then some.

Edith continued. "Your first assignment is to find out what the hell happened at that tennis club." Edith lit a cigarette that was fitted into a plastic holder. Did they still make those things? With typical disregard, Edith obviously didn't care that smoking inside was illegal in the office, and it didn't seem a good time to challenge her. She placed the thin cigarette between her lips. For emphasis, she took the holder in and out as she talked. "Are you being framed?" Puff. "Are you being used as a scapegoat?" Long, thoughtful puff. "Or, are you the killer?!" She took a puff of her cigarette and blew it in my face.

I was backing up towards the door, negotiating my escape. "You know I would never jeopardize The Bugle…on purpose." Now! Now! I said to myself. I quickly opened the door and scurried out.

I took a deep breath as I stood out in the hallway. My clothes were damp, palms sweaty and my hair…my hair had been touched by Edith. Roscoe darted out from the men's room.

"I'm gonna be digging up every dirty detail about you McGhie...until you're fired. Then, you'll know what it's like being rejected," Roscoe sneered.

I looked at the back of Roscoe's pants. Toilet paper was sticking out.

"Hey, Charlie. Is this guy giving you trouble" asked Wally.

Wally was our sports guy. He threw a basketball at Roscoe's stomach. "Catch, Minsk!"

"Ooph!" groaned Roscoe.

Roscoe wasn't a sports guy. He missed the ball and doubled over. I gave Wally a smile.

I called Robin from the car. "Hey, do you want to go to Mount Fuji tonight? I need to review that restaurant and I'm taking the kids."

"Sure. I'll meet you at Fuji's at 6:00," said Robin.

"See ya then!" I said. I hung up.

CHAPTER 4

It was 4 o'clock and Josh would be home from a neighbor's house in a few minutes. I made a mental note to pick up Jake up from a soccer game at 5:00. I decided to check my e-mail. My office was upstairs, next to my bedroom. I logged in. Before I did anything today, like get sent to jail, I wanted to find out if I was in the line-up for my New Jersey USTA team. And, I was. I was playing with Savannah. Good. I was consistent, and Savannah was a banshee at the net. We were a really strong team. The rest of the line-up looked pretty good. We were playing "The Volley Dollies." Dumb name...but they were a darn good team.

I didn't recognize another e-mail sent to me, but the subject matter was tennis, so I clicked on the letter icon. There was a picture sent as an attachment. I clicked on it. Ugh! It was a dead, bloody deer lying in the street. "You won't know what hit you." The caption read.

Should I tell the police about this? What would they do? They would probably think I was over-reacting. I pulled out officer Alex's card from today and started singing, "Matchmaker, matchmaker make me a match, find me a find, catch me a catch. Matchmaker, matchmaker look through your book and find me

31

the perfect match." I see a dead dear and start thinking about hooking up with Alex? What did that mean? Just then, the doorbell rang. It was Jake. Thank goodness he came home before I could sing a second verse.

I greeted him at the door with a hug and kiss. "Hi, handsome. How was school?"

"Boring. When are we going to Fuji's?" Jake asked.

"We're picking up Josh in an hour," I said.

"I'm gonna shoot hoops till you're ready," Jake said.

The phone rang. It was Alex. "Ms. McGhie?"

"Yes." My stomach knotted.

"We found traces of cyanide in those vials we found in your tennis bag," Alex said.

"In my tennis bag? Oh, right, those vials. Someone obviously put them there. I didn't poison her!" I said emphatically. "If you want, I'll take a lie detector test. Why would I want to kill Grace's team? Why would I want to poison mass quantities of people? I have two boys. Why would I want to jeopardize going to jail? You can't seriously think I'm a suspect in this…." I was so nervous, I couldn't stop talking.

"Ms. McGhie, Ms. McGhie." Alex finally interrupted. "We're not officially charging you yet, but you're still a person of interest. Could I give you some advice?"

"Yes, yes. Advice would be good. I need advice. I'm open to advice…" I was interrupted again.

"Shut up!" Alex said.

"That's your advice?" I was surprised.

"That's my advice," Alex said matter-of-factly. "Stop talking before you say something that could incriminate you. We're still interviewing people at the club."

It sounded like Alex was warming up to me…just a little.

"Okay. I'll shut up. Advice appreciated," I said.

"And, let me give you another bit of advice. Things aren't always how they appear." Alex hung up.

What does that mean? The doorbell rang. It was Marshall.

"I've come to pick up the kids," he said

"This isn't your weekend," I said nervously. Marshall always made me nervous. Especially now that he was suing me for full custody of the kids.

"Actually, it is. I have our agreement in the car, if you don't believe me," he said dismissively.

I took a step outside. Gayle was in the car. "Why did you bring her? She's practically a hooker. I don't want her around the kids."

"Gayle's a dancer, Charlie. You know that. She could probably teach you a few moves," he laughed.

"I'm sure she could, as long as it involves a pole and a 10 dollar bill," I said. I made the Joan Rivers, "uh, uh, uh" sound and vomit motion with my fingers. "Listen, just let me take the kids to Fuji tonight. The boys are really looking forward to going before overnight camp starts."

"Which is when?" he asked.

"Saturday!" I gave him the eye roll. He wants custody and he barely knows what's going on in their lives. "Then, I'll drop them off at your house."

"I expect to see you at 8 o'clock sharp," Marshall said disgustedly. "Or else, I'll make sure the judge hears that you broke the agreement."

I saw him give Jake a hug and a high five on the driveway. I felt like I was having a nervous breakdown. When Marshall finds out that I'm being implicated for murder and that someone was trying to kill me, he would go right to the judge and take away my kids for good.

CHAPTER 5

Mount Fuji was the only restaurant where my kids ate everything on their plate and more. If I looked away while I was eating, they would eat my food and it probably wouldn't take much for them to eat their neighbor's food at the communal table. Both Josh and Jake were still mesmerized by the corny hibachi show, even though they'd seen it thousands of times. When we walked in, the place was bustling. I was, of course, wearing a disguise. Tonight I was going with an Island look: a Rastafarian dreadlock wig, matched smartly with an Island Moo Moo. I usually wore a disguise when I was critiquing a restaurant. I didn't want special treatment or the food being extra special because I was a reviewer. My kids stopped being embarrassed by my sometimes outlandish outfits, years ago. Robin happened to be going to a Wicca meeting after dinner, so she was wearing her high priestess coat. A large pentagram pendent hung prominently around her neck. Although born Jewish, Robin started studying Wicca after her mother passed away too young because of a doctor's careless mistake. Unfortunately, the same thing happened to my mother and Robin and I had formed a strong bond of friendship because of it.

Our table was full. It was a large rectangle with a hibachi grill in the middle. After a waiter took our drink and dinner order, the chef came wearing his chef's hat with a big indent on top to catch the eggs he would throw up.

"Gooh evanin," said the chef. The chef didn't smile. He seemed agitated. He exchanged sharp words, in Japanese, with our waitress. She angrily answered him right back as she plunked down our drinks. He sharpened his gigantic knives as he glared at her. He began to slice an onion, then squirted it with lighter fluid and the whole table burst into flames. The kids around the table squealed with delight. The chef proceeded to put out the flame with a squirt toy that looked like a boy. Yes, it was a "boy toy." The water came out of the boy's penis when the chef squeezed the toy. "Wee wee," said the chef. The chef playfully squirted random people at the table. He looked at me.

"Wee wee, not me," I said.

For the chef's next trick, he moved the onion across the grill (with his knife), while playing a flute that sounded like a train whistle. He then began cooking the huge pile of white rice. He took out two eggs and rolled them across the grill. "Egg woll," said the chef. He then cracked the eggs, threw the empty shells up and caught them in the middle of his hat. He then threw two slabs of butter onto the grill. "Japanese 'butter fly'." For his last trick, the chef cut up 5 shrimp into tiny pieces. He went around the large table trying to throw pieces of shrimp into people's mouths. Nobody caught the shrimp. My shrimp missed my mouth completely and got stuck in one of my dreadlocks. My kids couldn't stop laughing. As Robin immediately turned to help get the shrimp out of my "hair," her shrimp wound up in her ear.

"Shit!" said Robin. "Can you get the shrimp out?" I was a little nearsighted, and almost had my nose in her ear, looking for the microscopic shrimp. One of my dreadlocks dipped into her wine.

"Oh, Robin, I'm so sorry!" I said. Suddenly, we both burst out laughing.

As we all ate dinner, I started to think that maybe the kids would be better off with Marshall. What kind of mother wears disguises to restaurants? Even though Jake was class president at his elementary school, I had never even been to a PTO meeting. Also, Josh had a million soccer awards, but I didn't have a "Soccer mom" sticker on the back of my car. The truth was, I wasn't very good at being a suburban mom. I was scattered and disorganized and, oh yeah…I also had a lunatic after me who was trying to kill me and frame me for murder. This isn't going to sit too kindly with all those PTO Moms.

I think I also dressed a little too trendy. I didn't own one pair of "mom" jeans. I didn't drive a van, and I was a disaster at craft projects.

Suddenly, I felt Jake's little hand slip into mine, under the table. "Love you, Mom!" said Jake. And he kissed me on the cheek.

"I love you too, Jake," I whispered right back to him.

"You're the best Mom ever," Jake said.

I shivered. It was like he was reading my mind. "I needed that. Thanks, Jakie."

I felt someone tap me on the shoulder. "Hi, Charlie." It was Steffi Scapelli. Steffi used to be my tennis partner several years ago.

"I heard you murdered Grace Denunzio," she said.

"Don't believe everything you hear," I said, channeling Alex.

"The Mood Swings" think you've snapped. "You killing Grace is payback for Grace having you sit during districts last year."

"Steffi, any sane person doesn't kill another person over tennis! Actually, any sane person doesn't kill another person, period. Listen to how ridiculous that sounds: me killing Grace."

Steffi snapped my picture with her cell-phone. "Just in case you did it. I could sell your picture on eBay."

"I guess the next thing you'll want me to do is sign it," I said.

"Would you? " asked Steffi

"Steffi, you're crazy," I said.

"I'm crazy? Hey, you're the one wearing the dreadlocks and a moo moo outfit," Steffi laughed. Thankfully, she walked away.

"C'mon, guys, let's go get some ice cream before I drop you off at Dad's," I said.

"What did she mean when she said you killed someone. Did you? Did you kill someone at tennis?" Asked Josh.

"She meant I beat Grace. I "killed" her in tennis. It's a figure of speech. Let's go get some ice cream. Robin, do you want to go??

"Sounds tempting, but I'm going to a singles Wiccan mixer."

"I hope you meet someone," I said. "At least you're going to a party where you have things in common with everyone."

But Robin looked glum. "Oh, let's just call it what it is. A bunch of desperate 40 somethings exchanging candles with men with dangling wicks."

"Mom, what does Aunt Robin mean? What's a dangling wick?" Josh smiled…way too loud. He darn knew what it meant.

I gave Robin the evil eye. Hopefully, she wouldn't use it against me. "Let's let Aunt Robin explain that."

"Well, uh, it's just a figure of speech. A dangling wick is really just another name for a candle, I mean, a man who can't make a commitment."

I was perspiring so much now I took off my wig. Jake and Josh were laughing.

"What's so funny?" I asked.

"Aunt Robin's going to a party where the men are so old they can't get a hard-on," said Jake. "That's why she said they have dangling wicks."

Way too loud. The restaurant became silent and everyone stared at us…everyone, including Marshall who had just walked in. He grabbed Josh and Jake by the hand.

"You're toast, Charlie. What kind of language are you teaching these kids? You'll be lucky to get visitation rights to ever see them again. Have a nice evening with your desperate, witch friend," said Marshall.

I ran outside after them. "Hey! Marshall! I was supposed to have the kids till 8:00! Jake was just making a joke."

Marshall already had the kids in his truck.

"Charlie, I'm so sorry. It's all my fault," said Robin.

"Wait till Marshall finds out I'm a murder suspect. If Wally has his way, I'll be the lead story in the Bugle tomorrow," I said.

"You're a person of interest. There's a difference," Robin said.

"You sound like Alex. You know we live in a small, gossipy town. I, I need to clear myself, quickly. Or, I might never see my kids again." I broke down in tears

.

CHAPTER 6

It was Saturday morning. Today, I would be going out incognito. I was not doing a review, but I needed to visit Bradley undetected. As a possible murder suspect, I wasn't sure whether I would be followed. I put on a brown wig, black sleeveless shirt, denim Capri's, ballet flats, a stylish scarf and big, black sunglasses. I made myself believe that I was an Audrey Hepburn stylish sleuth….from *Charade*, I thought. I was in command, like the equally stylish Jackie-O. Look good, act smart and walk in the shadows….like that girl in West Side Story who wanted to be a Jet. And, whatever I did, I must not read today's paper. I needed to talk to Bradley. I needed advice on how to clear myself and how to track down the real killer.

I got in my RAV4 and put on the radio. "…..and that's the latest update on Charlie McGhie, a food critic, with what seems like "a 'taste' for crime! Back to you, Jack." I snapped off the radio. "A taste for crime, indeed!" Think, think, think. Who would have had a chance to spike the soup? Everyone, duh. It could have been anyone who was working the desk, any of the pros, Henry, the weirdo stringer, people watching the matches…

"And the list is endless, Bradley. It's going to be impossible to find out who did it." I looked at poor, pathetic Bradley. My problems seemed small compared to his. He was still in a full body cast with one leg and one arm elevated on a pulley contraption. "I brought you a present. A scratcher thing." I took out the long, thin, plastic bar with a hand on the end.

"Could you get my nose?" I scratched his nose.

"And, could you get under my arm?" I slid the hand under his arm cast. "Thanks."

"What am I going to do?" I asked.

"Anyone have any grudges against you?" Bradley asked in earnest.

"Yes, everyone who plays tennis. I can't tell you how many people I've pissed off over the years."

"Anyone you know that would have access to poison?"

"I don't know about poison. But, we have a team dealer."

"A team dealer?" Bradley gave me the same "horror/disgust" look that Alex gave me when we first talked.

"Yeah. Barb Calhoun. Her husband's an exec in a pharmaceutical company. She always has samples of everything. But, I don't think she would have access to poison," I said.

"Hmm, you never know who would plant poison in your handbag."

"Well, I don't know where to start looking for suspects."

Bradley sang, "Start at the very beginning, it's a very good place to start…"

"Geez. Bradley. You're not taking this seriously."

"You need to start…."

I took out my notebook. The next sound out of Bradley's mouth was loud snoring. I tiptoed out of the room, and quickly made my way to the elevator.

As I was about to hit the elevator button, another hand beat me to it. Alex's. Once inside the elevator, he began grilling me.

"I thought you told me everything you knew about Grace."

"I did."

"Grace was your ex-husband's lawyer, and his wife's sister. Grace was working on giving Marshall complete child custody for Jake and Josh."

"So."

"So, now there is real motive for you killing her. You were angry. You wanted revenge. Why didn't you tell me? You knew we were going to find that out sooner or later. Plus, there still is the small matter of finding three vials of cyanide in your hand bag."

"I'm having a nervous breakdown. Can you give me a break? I know things don't look good. Do you have kids?"

"No", said Alex.

"Well, my kids mean everything to me. Marshall is taking me to court for being an unfit mother. He wants to take my kids away from me. Do you know what that is doing to me?"

"Why does he think you're an unfit mother?"

"Because I'm unorganized, a clutter-bug, clean laundry always needs to be put away, and I don't have their soccer schedules memorized, etc, etc. Marshall is anal retentive and vindictive. It's an unfortunate combination. Plus, I work full-time at the Bucks Bugle, so I'm not home when the kids get home from school. Marshall hates that."

"How old are your kids?"

"Jake is 10 and Josh is 14."

"So, what's the real reason he wants custody? Your kids seem old enough to let themselves into the house. And clutter? That's not a crime."

"I caught him in a lie. Josh was sick and I needed to take him to the emergency room. So, I called Marshall at a friend's house, where I thought he was playing cards. I found out he was with an exotic dancer…his current wife."

"Sounds like he just wants to make your life miserable."

"He's succeeding. And, once the court finds out I'm wanted for murder…"

"Allegedly wanted for murder," Alex corrected.

"The court is bound to say I'm an unfit mother. Listen, do you want to go get a coffee?"

"I, I can't."

"Not interested in mixing with an alleged felon?"

"You don't scare me. Actually, dating a criminal could be a turn-on. But, I have a girlfriend."

"You are a rare breed, Alex. You have integrity and morals."

"Actually, I just have a really jealous girlfriend."

I took a good look at Alex. We were outside now. He had outstanding features: shiny brown hair, ocean-blue eyes, a tall, slim build and an easy-going smile. Damn! Why were the good ones always taken?

"I'm really sorry I have a girlfriend, if that means anything."

Wow, and he has ESP, too. This guy has it all.

"Try and keep a low profile. We're still questioning people who were at the club that day."

Jitters was hopping. I finally found a small corner table. Drinking my decaf skim, mocha latte, I was mulling over Alex's parting words when I suddenly felt a finger tap me on the shoulder. It was Jazzy.

"I'm glad I ran into you. I have something to tell you, but it's gotta be in the vault. If my teammates knew I was even talking to you, I'd be kicked off the team. And, who knows if we're being watched, or if you're bugged..."

"What is it, Jazzy?" She reminded me of a yapping Chihuahua.

"You first have to tell me that it's in the vault."

"It's in the vault."

"You swear you're not gonna tell anyone?"

"Jazzy. Vault."

"I have a prime suspect for you, Nora Westfield. She could have planted the poison in your purse and the soup."

"Nora?" I was extremely skeptical.

"You know that the Westfields are getting divorced," Jazzy whispered.

The Westfields were the owner's of Mill Creek.

"No, I didn't know that." I was shocked. Not that the Westfield's were getting divorced, but that I hadn't heard a major piece of tennis gossip.

"It's nasty," Jazzy continued. "They're fighting over the club."

"But, everyone knows that they're in debt over the club and the club is falling apart. Why would Nora want the club? It doesn't make sense."

"Assets, baby. It's all about assets. Even though they haven't paid off their mortgage, she could still sell the club and make a huge profit."

"Okay, if that's true, why would she plant poison in my handbag, tennis bag or maybe even spike the soup I made? It doesn't make sense. If anything, she could be ruining the club's reputation and, oh, that would also make her an accessory to a crime."

"Gary is winning. The property is in his name. Nora's out to sabotage him now."

"How do you know all this?"

"I can't tell you, it's in the vault.

"I don't believe you."

"Chad told me, alright? And…"

"It's in the vault, I know. But, how would Chad know?"

"He let it slip when we were…you know."

"You and Chad?" Why not me and Chad? What did Jazzy have that I didn't have? Ka-ching…that's what. Chad was a money whore. Jazzy took lessons from him twice a week. "I don't believe you."

"Well, do you believe this?" Jazzy lifted up her ponytail to reveal a very large hickey.

"What are you…like twelve?"

"You're just jealous, Charlie. Chad's unbelievable in bed."

"Speak of the devil," I said. We both looked as Chad walked through the door. He was on his cell phone and didn't even notice us.

"Café mocha and a scone," said Chad. "Lots of whipped cream."

I looked at Jazzy. "Don't even go there.

Chad finally noticed us and walked over. "What's up, you two?"

"I don't know, why don't you tell me what's up?" I asked as I glanced at Jazzy's neck

Chad blushed. I cringed; Jazzy was telling the truth.

"Any news about how Grace died?" Chad asked.

"The editor at my paper thinks I did it because Grace didn't play me in Districts last summer. Have you ever heard anything more ridiculous?"

"You were on Grace's team last summer?" Chad was surprised.

Just then Jazzy's partner, Collette, walked through the door. "Ca va, Jazzy?"

It was 90 degrees outside and she was wearing a damn scarf wrapped around her neck. She held a pack of cigarettes in her hand. How did the French do it? They smoke, they drank, they ate fat, yet they were all thin, had low cholesterol and were genetically fashionable.

"How are you doing, Charlie?"

"Things could be better, Collette. If you'll excuse me."

Chad guided me out the door and onto the cobblestone sidewalk. "I just want to say that I don't think you did it."

"And why is that? Did you sleep with Jazzy, by the way?"

"I don't kiss and tell. So, when are you going to have a private with me?"

I laughed. "Don't you know that nothing with you is private?"

"Tennis gossip is much worse on the East Coast than the West Coast. It's not my fault. I hope you'll schedule a private. There's a lot we could work on." He smiled.

"My game's that bad, huh?

"No, you've got a good game, just a few things need to be tweaked."

I looked at him funny. "You have become a walking double entendre." I stared at him again, feeling very awkward. And, I never felt awkward around him probably because it was becoming harder and harder to deny that, I too, had a crush on him. He had the requisite good looks of a touring pro: dirty blonde tousled hair, blue eyes, easy smile, tall and taut. I was only human, for goodness sake. I must have said this last part out loud.

"What do you mean 'you're only human'?" Chad asked.

"Oh! I mean that, uh, all the pressure of being under suspicion is really getting to me. So, why don't you think I did it?

"Too many people around. Anyone could have tampered with the soup. Did anyone help you make it?

"No."

"Who carried it into the club?"

"Me. Wait a minute, Barb carried the crockpot. She was helping me in the parking lot."

"Hmm."

"Hmm, meaning you think Barb might have done it?"

"She did have access. At this point, anyone could be a suspect."

"And the cyanide capsules found in my purse?" I asked.

"Hmm," Chad pondered again.

Nothing was coming after the second "hmm." I knew that this second piece of evidence could be seen as irrefutably damning.

Chad pulled out his cell phone. "I've got a lesson in 15 minutes...I've got to go."

As he walked down the sidewalk, I saw several women stare at him. Snap out of it, McGhie. Chad's out of your league. Just focus on clearing yourself, because nothing else matters if you don't.

CHAPTER 7

I was passing Prudence's office, when I heard Prudence singing, "Who's peekin' out from under a stairway, calling a name that's lighter than air? Who's bending down to give me a rainbow, everyone knows it's Windy."

"Prudence?"

"Oh, hi Charlie."

"What's going on?"

"What do you mean?"

"I mean, 'And Windy has stor-my eyes, that flash at the sound of lies'…"

"Oh, you heard me, huh?"

"Uh, yeah."

Prudence started panicking. "Please don't tell Edith."

"That you're singing 'Windy'?"

"I have an audition at YNOT. They're looking for a new weather person. And, I thought…" Prudence made the quote marks. "'Y NOT' me? I'm pretty, I'm perky, and there's no one who knows weather better than me."

"So, why are you singing 'Windy'?" I still wasn't making the connection.

"Windy is weather, Charlie. I thought it would be cute and different if I had a song that introduced me. Like baseball

46

players have when they're introduced onto the field. Windy is the perfect song for me: it's fun, it's upbeat, and it screams, weather."

"Good luck. But, I would close your door if you're going to sing."

As I left Prudence's office, I wondered what I wondered each day at work: Why did Prudence get the office and I got the cubicle? No feeling sorry for myself, I had work to do. I made myself a cup of coffee, grabbed a donut, today's Bucks Bugle and did what I did best: made a list. I was a great list maker. The more time it took me to make a list, the greater time I had to procrastinate. Let's see… 1. Call Alex to find out if there was any info on Grace's autopsy. Check on Bucky's autopsy, too. 2. Find out if there were any lab results on the soup. 3. Interview everyone that was at the tennis match that had a motive…especially Maria's husband, Dal. Now that he was allowed to talk, maybe he would be anxious to spill the beans as it were. I smiled at my bad pun. Dal was a vegetarian. Wait a minute, what motive would a monk have? I was losing my mind. 4. I gasped. Just then Robin poked her head in.

"Making lists again? Why did you gasp?"

"Maybe Marshall spiked the soup. I had made the soup the night before and put it in a Tupperware in the refrigerator. Then, I was out for several hours shopping with the kids. He has keys to the house. Marshall's a doctor, Robin. He probably knows all about poison."

"He's a dermatologist, not a mad scientist. Just because he's a doctor, doesn't mean he would have access to poison. I don't think Marshall is quite as Machiavellian as you're making him out to be. Grace was a heavy woman. She could have had any number of health problems, like an arrhythmia, high cholesterol, high blood pressure, heart disease."

"I haven't told you this, but I think I'm being followed…like everywhere."

My phone rang. "Charlie McGhie," I answered. I felt the color drain from my face. "We agreed to split custody, Marshall….uh huh…uh huh…uh huh." Thwack! I slammed the phone down. "Marshall's lawyer filed a petition for permanent custody because there's probable cause that I committed a murder…and the court agreed!" I broke down and cried.

"Charlie, I'm so sorry. Let me see your list. Did you call Alex?" Robin said.

"Alex has been tailing me."

"Tailing you? I see you've got the lingo down."

My phone rang again. "Marshall, if you don't stop harassing me, I'm going to call the cops…oh, hi Officer Alex. Boy, that was quick. Need a cop and there you are. (pause) I've lost temporary custody of my kids. I don't think I can take anymore bad news. (pause) I'm hanging in there, thanks. Bye."

Robin raised her eyebrows.

"Don't look at me like that," I said. "He has a girlfriend."

"He likes you. He doesn't need to call and see how you're doing. Especially, because you're supposed to be a suspect."

"He thinks I've been framed."

Just then Roscoe poked his head in. "Just came by to give you some good news. The police think Bucky was poisoned. I didn't know that you were a hamster hater, McGhie."

"And, why is that good news?" I asked.

"Because maybe, somehow, the hamster and Grace are connected. Maybe the same person…YOU…poisoned them both."

"I have no motive, Roscoe. I'm not crazy about hamsters, but I would never kill one. And, I wasn't at school at the time of the….murder. And, I didn't kill Grace. Besides, the police won't really know until an autopsy is done."

Roscoe sat on my desk. Just then, Edith walked by.

"Is this a coffee klatch? Do you three need more work? Break it up." She clapped her hands.

A coffee klatch? Where's the typing pool? Edith was reliving the glory days of the 50's classic, "The Best of Everything." Now she's Joan Crawford's Amanda Farrow.

"Charlie, I need you to review 'Sacre Bleu!' tonight." It's that new French restaurant in New Hope."

"But, I thought I was an investigative reporter now."

"Two hats, Charlie." Edith was tapping my head. "I need you to wear two hats now. Just till Bradley gets on his feet."

"Poor Bradley," we all said in unison.

Edith left and I stuck a tack into Roscoe's hand.

"Ow!" What are you, a sadist?"

"Off my desk, Minsk!"

Roscoe took off his tie and wrapped his hand. "I'm telling Edith." Thankfully, he left.

"What a baby," I said to Robin. "By the way, how was that party you went to the other night. Did you meet anyone?"

"I did. His name is Phil and he's a warlock. But, he's a little, uh...dark."

"Dark?"

"Depressing."

"What does he do?"

"He's an exterminator."

I looked at her.

"I know. Killing bugs and rodents all day is enough to depress anyone. But, he's really cute, owns his own company and plays a mean game of Charades."

"Would you and Phil like to go with me to Sacre Bleu!, tonight?"

"Thanks, Charlie. I'll ask him. What about the kids?

"Marshall has them. I'll see you there at 7:00."

"I almost forgot." Robin rummaged through her purse and pulled out a candle and a small vial. "This is a candle for protection and I want you to dress it with this. Just pour it on the candle, before you light it, visualize yourself surrounded by white light. I'm worried about you."

"Me, too," said Alex. Alex popped his head over the cubicle.

"Hello, Officer Alex. What brings you to my humble cubicle?"

"I'll see you later, Charlie," said Robin, mouthing "He's cute!" behind his back.

Just then my cell phone beeped. It was a text.

"Aren't you going to look at it?" Alex asked.

"No."

"Why?"

"I've been getting threatening texts."

"What do they say?"

"'Stop digging or you'll be lucky to see the morning.' That's one of the sweeter ones."

"Have you called back any of the numbers?"

"It's a different 800 number each time."

"I want you to start writing down the numbers."

"I've already been doing that. I was going to put them through Nexus." I showed him the piece of paper with the numbers.

"Let me know what you find out."

My eyes started to well up again. "I'm sorry, I just don't know what I've done for someone to want to target me like this. I'm a composter, for God's sake. Do you think whoever it is would do anything to my kids?"

"What are you doing tonight?"

"A date? Have you broken up with the girlfriend?"

"No, I just want to keep an eye on you."

"I'm supposed to review a French restaurant, "Sacre Bleu!." Robin and her boyfriend are meeting me there. Do you want to come with me?"

"I'll meet you there."

"So, why did you stop by?"

"We found Grace's PDA. Actually, one of the pros did at the club. I wanted you to look at printouts of the calendars for these past months and her reminder notes. See if anything looks suspicious to you." Alex handed me several sheets of paper.

I scoured the sheets. "Nothing jumps out at me, except she does seem to be very social with her team…but that's not weird. Of course, I only like one or two people on my team. There are several names and numbers that I don't know. Did you speak with Grace's team? I really wasn't that friendly with her."

"They've already looked at these sheets. Nothing."

"Wait a minute, this looks like a European number. England? It begins with 01. And, she has lots of memos to call 'Terry' at weird times.' Who's Terry? Terry must be English."

"We're in the process of doing a check on that number. Did Grace have a boyfriend? She wasn't married."

"I'm not sure. You should talk to Plug, she was Grace's partner."

"Plug?"

"Lilly Wurthenheim. They were inseparable."

"So, how do you know that it wasn't me who did it."

"I don't. I'll pick you up at 6:45."

Alex turned to leave.

"A date! I smiled with satisfaction."

"It's not a date."

"I thought you were meeting me there?"

Alex just smiled at me and left..

CHAPTER 8

When I got home from work, the kids were packing to stay with their dad. I couldn't keep from crying. Both boys hugged me. I thought how lucky I was to have two teenage boys who were both so warm. No one said anything. What could we say? They didn't understand why they had to leave and I certainly didn't understand either. I couldn't say, "Staying with your dad is the right thing to do", because it wasn't. It was a vindictive thing that Marshall was doing. And the pole dancer he was married to was certainly no role model. I needed a lawyer. I really needed to clear myself. This whole thing was ridiculous. A bad episode of "Murder She Wrote." You know what, I needed Jessica Fletcher.

Just then, the doorbell rang. I looked out the window. It was Marshall.

"I'm hoping it's only for a couple of days," I said to my boys.

Both boys hugged me again and told me they loved me. I helped them down the stairs with their suitcases, backpacks and books.

"Don't forget to brush…." I said as I opened the door.

Marshall glared at me as he picked up the suitcases.

"You're going to regret this Marshall. You know this whole thing is a misunderstanding. You know I'm not a murderer."

"Tell that to my lawyer. Oh, that's right, you can't. You killed her!"

And he shut the door in my face.

A minute later the doorbell rang again. I opened it up and said, "Fuck you!"

"I know you didn't mean that in the biblical sense," said Alex

"Well, currently, yes. Marshall just took the kids. He got custody because of this stupid misunderstanding. Let's go."

Sacre Bleu! was hopping. All the beautiful people from Philly were there: celebrity newscasters, local television stars, even Sharon Pincus, head of the Philly film board. And, then there was the tennis crowd, a mix of various tennis friends and foes. Every table was filled and the bar was packed. Alex led me to the bar.

"I'm going to need to elbow a few people to get a drink," I said.

"Just tell them that you play tennis and they should be scared…very scared," smiled Alex.

We both laughed. Two people left their stools and we grabbed their seats.

"I'll have a Cosmopolitan," I said to the bartender.

"Vodka on the rocks with a twist," said Alex.

Half way through my Cosmo, I saw Robin and Phil. Phil seemed to be looking at the walls and floor as he walked…like he was looking for something. We waved.

"Hi! Sorry we're late. Charlie, Officer Alex, this is my friend, Phil."

"Nice to meet you," Alex said.

"Phil, it looked like you were looking for something when you walked in," I said.

"I exterminated this place today, " whispered Phil. "They have mice."

"They have mice here?" The woman sitting next to me looked alarmed.

A woman standing overheard the woman.

"There're mice here? But, this restaurant just opened."

"Ooh!" said another woman. "Gross!" said her friend.

And soon the Sacre Bleu! bar buzz turned from appetizer talk to infestation worry.

The four of us quickly slunk away and tried to become anonymous in the crowd.

"Let's find out if our table is ready," I said.

We bobbed and weaved our way toward the Maître 'D. He looked annoyed as he surveyed the diners then studied his seating chart. My guess was that people were lingering too long at their tables and messing up the seating times. He erased then drew numbers in at different tables. Finally, he sat us at a small round table in the middle of the restaurant. As we sat down, I saw Plug sitting at the table next to us. I gave her a fake smile and she fake smiled right back at me.

Three waiters were assigned to our table: one to refold and replace our napkins, one to replenish our water glasses, and one to take our order. The menu was both interesting and appropriately French-intricate. Phil still looked jittery and unable to concentrate on the menu.

"I need to check the kitchen," Phil said. "I've been seeing some little presents, if you know what I mean."

We all knew what he meant; and it certainly wasn't a meal enhancer.

"You must have pretty good vision, Phil," said Alex.

"Well, it's helpful for my day job."

"Do you have a night job?"

"I work at the "Kabbalah & Kibbutz" coffee shop in New Hope, a few nights a week. We also sell candles, oils, books and various bric-a-brac."

"Phil's a warlock," Robin gushed. "He's amazing."

Alex's raised eyebrows gave me all the assurance I needed that he thought we were all lunatics.

"You know, I wouldn't mind seeing the kitchen myself. When I review a restaurant, I always like to see the kitchen. C'mon, Phil, let's find the owner."

Just then, a waiter came to take our order.

"I'll have the escargot to start, the vichyssoise, and poached halibut," I said.

"I'm going to have the French onion soup and the steak with pomme frittes," said Phil.

I grabbed Phil's hand and tugged him away from the table. "Iksnay on the arlockway," I said, looking for the kitchen.

"I gather Alex isn't a believer," said Phil.

"Alex Tevyalexski is a cop, need I say more."

We were about to enter the kitchen when we were stopped by the owner, Marc Naduce.

"No one is allowed in the kitchen."

"Hi, I'm Phil. I'm an exterminator and exterminated your restaurant this morning."

The manager just looked at him.

"Mice."

"Oui, mice," said Marc.

"Well, I think you still have quite a few mice, from what I've seen. I was hoping to take a look at your kitchen. I have some poisoned peanut butter cubes and some traps in my car."

Marc took out a wad of bills.

"I can't take that," Phil said.

"Messier, this is opening night. If anyone found out about these mouse traps, it would close our business like that!" He imitated a snapping trap with his hands. "We would be the mice, caught in bad publicity. And, who are you?" Marc turned to me.

"I'm Charlotte McGhie, restaurant reviewer for the Bucks Bugle." I was wondering if he was going to offer me a wad of cash. I wasn't as proud as Phil.

"Merde! Merde! An exterminator with a food critic, how could I be so unlucky...tonight of all nights. You can have a quick look, but do not touch anything."

Phil seemed to look at every crevice and crack in the kitchen. I was taking note of kitchen hygiene, technique and ingredients used in the dishes. Phil was shaking his head and sighing when we left the kitchen. "They've got friends in small places."

I laughed. "That's a very funny exterminator joke."

When we got back to our seats, our first course was being served, only Phil and I received the mushroom bisque, Alex received the onion soup, not having ordered soup and Robin got an order of mussels in white wine.

"This obviously isn't our order. We need to find one of our three waiters," I said.

Our waiters were huddled around Plug's table. Charlie Brown said it best, "Good grief."

They quickly came back to our table, gathered up the plates and ushered the food over to the other table.

"That's many demerits," I said, writing in my little black reviewers book. They should have given the other table fresh food."

All of a sudden we heard a curdling scream coming from Plug's table. Her head was floating in her soup. Everyone in the restaurant started screaming. Alex immediately got up from the table and ran to Plug's table. He called 911 on his walkie-talkie. Photographers swarmed around Plug's table. But, because I was a recently alleged murderer, they were taking pictures of my table, too. The soup that killed Plug was served to our table first, so now my friends were also suspects..

CHAPTER 9

The silence of our jail cell was broken by the familiar click-clack of high heels. I knew that sound anywhere.

Our cell was opened and Edith threw a newspaper at our heads. The headline read, "SACRE BLEU! SERVES DEADLY WITCHES BREW!" There was a picture of me, Robin and Phil looking like three startled deer.

"Robin, if you want to use one of your poisoned potions on someone on your own time, that's your business, but when it effects the reputation of The Bucks Bugle, well, that's my business. What am I going to do with you two?"

"Edith, I know this doesn't look good," I said.

"Two hats, Charlie. I asked you to wear two hats. I didn't think that one of them was going to be black and pointy."

"I didn't poison the soup. I don't even know how to cast a spell or use potions."

Robin was shaking her head. "It's the truth, Edith. If anyone should be in trouble, it's me. Charlie doesn't know anything about potions."

"A soup sample came back from the lab with the oils that you had left on Charlie's desk. Toxic oils that you had given Charlie for her candle were poured in Lilly's soup."

Robin and I gasped. "The oils for the candle? Who would have taken that vial?" asked Robin. "Who knew Charlie even had that vial?"

"Roscoe!" We both said in unison. "Alex!" we said a beat later.

"Anybody could have walked by your desk and seen that vial sitting there," said Edith.

"But not many people would know what that vial was or even pay attention to it. It's so small," said Robin. "By the way, where's Phil?"

"I got him out, too. They're ready!" Edith said to the guard. We gingerly walked out of the cell. The warden was standing with the guard. Was that a wink I saw the warden give Edith?

In the car, I could tell from Edith's uneasy voice, that my job was on the line.

"Two poisonings in two weeks. No more reviews for you until we get to the bottom of this. Prudence will be taking over your column."

"Prudence?! I went to culinary school and had my own catering business for 10 years. What credentials does Prudence have?"

"How about that she hasn't killed anyone."

"I'm an 'alleged' killer. You can't possibly think I murdered two people. I have no motive." I was very tempted to tell Edith that Prudence was looking for a TV gig, but out of a stupid loyalty, I did not. It seemed like sweet Prudence was anything but. She was really a ruthless backstabber. And, maybe...an accessory to a murder? She saw those vials of oils on my desk. She even commented that she wanted Phil to make her a money candle. Was she in debt? Did she want to get back at me for some reason?

"Grace was representing your ex-husband in your custody battle. And what about the 'DQ' nonsense that Roscoe was babbling on about? Together, they're a powerful motive. Look, the only reason I haven't fired you is that Bugle sales have been up since the two poisonings. It's all about the numbers, Charlie. Your notoriety is keeping the Bugle afloat."

I kept my mouth shut. I needed the money. I couldn't wait to get to my computer. I had a huge to-do list.

As I walked through the Bugle doors, I tried to keep my head held high. But, everyone was staring at me. Prudence was at the copy machine.

"Gray skies are gonna clear up…put on a happy face," sang Prudence.

The rest of the office chimed in: "And, spread sunshine, all over the place, just put on a happy face!"

"Shut up, Prudence!" I was in no mood for her weather songs. Traitor! "Can I talk with you for a minute?"

"In my office or your cubicle?" Prudence smiled.

"If I had a door it would be my cubicle. And now I don't even have my column."

Prudence looked a little nervous. "Hey, I think you made a wood pun."

"A wood pun?"

"Door…column"

I shut the door to her office.

"Did you or did you not ask Phil to make you a money candle?"

"I did."

"Did you or did you not know what that vial was for on my desk?"

"I did."

"Well, someone took it and dumped it in Plug's soup."

"I know, Charlie. But, I didn't do it."

"You were looking for a TV gig. Are you in debt?"

"I'm not getting paid more for taking over your column. If anything, it's going to be a pain in the ass. Like I told you, I want to be on TV. I want to be an actress. Why would I try and frame you…it doesn't make any sense."

"None of this makes sense."

"Who would benefit by putting you in jail?"

"My ex-husband." My ex? The thought did cross my mind. He would do anything to get custody of the kids. But, implicate me in a murder?

"Marshall could have hired a hit man to do it…so his hands would be clean," Prudence said, a bit too convincingly.

Prudence took a cigar out of her desk, lit it, opened her window, and put her feet up. I was stunned.

"I have to be honest, I thought you were a ditzy weather girl," I said.

"Oh, I'm still ditzy," Prudence was puffing away. "But, lately I've been watching a lot of Murder She Wrote reruns. "Who's the least likely person you think who'd do it….and that is who probably did it."

"I've already tried channeling Jessica Fletcher. It doesn't work. But, that could be you…or Robin…or Alex, or Phil, or Jen…or Savannah…. No, Savannah's too preoccupied with sex to plan a murder. It could be a hundred different people. I'll see you later, Pru."

I stumbled out of Prudence's office deep in thought. Not deep enough that I didn't pick up two chocolate donuts and a hot cup of coffee on the way to my cubicle. That's three donuts so far today, which is about…900 calories?

I picked up a legal pad as I munched. I drew a vertical line down the middle. I wrote TENNIS CLUB on one side and SACRE BLEU on the other. I started writing down the names that were at each poisoning, hoping that I would see a connection. I looked at my candle that Robin had given me….for protection. Hmm. Some protection. I picked up the Bucks Bugle and looked in the Obit page, wondering if there was a write-up of Plug. Bonanza! Not only was Plug's viewing tomorrow afternoon, but so was Bucky the hamster's. They were giving the hamster a viewing….well, not a viewing; it looks like Bucky was Jewish: "Bucky Birnbaum, beloved hamster is survived by his parents Scott and Andrea Birnbaum and his sister Melissa and brother Justin." I wonder if Melissa and Justin were hamsters or people? "There will be a gravesite service at the Shalom Cemetery in Doylestown."

My cell-phone beeped. A text from Savannah: Hey missy prissy, don't 4get match 2-morrow at 10. Have not hrd from u in days! R u in love xxxx? I texted back: hardly. been in jail will explain when I c u. Do u no who we r playing?" "Got Balls?"…and looking forward to c-ing if they do!" she texted back. "Take a shower" I replied.

Maybe now was a good time to take a private with Chad. I could find out if he's heard any Mill Creek gossip and work on my serve and volley at the same time. I called Mill Creek. Luckily, Chad had a cancellation and could fit me in at 2:00. Perfect. I could take a lesson and then I needed to finish ironing on labels and packing the boys trunks for overnight camp.

"Hey, any word on how Bradley's doing?" I was standing on my desk, leaning over my cubicle partition. Inge was typing away on her computer.

"Haven't you heard?" Inge responded with her heavy German accent.

Like everyone's heard but me.

"Heard?" I asked.

"He's in hiding," Inge replied.

"Hiding?"

"Why do you keep repeating vhat I'm saying?" Inge sounded annoyed.

I bent down and peeled the paper of an errant straw on my desk. I stood up again and shot a spitball at Inge. And, then I locked eyes with Edith. Uh, oh.

"Charlie!" Edith yelled.

"I'm de-stressing, Edith."

"Can you move her?" Inge asked Edith. "I'm on deadline, and she's always…doing stupid zings to me."

"She's already been moved three times. There's no where else for her to go." Edith sighed, exasperated.

Talking about me in 3rd person. Hmmph. "How about a real office," I asked. "If I'm completely enclosed, I won't bother anyone. There's too much temptation to annoy in cubicles."

"I never thought I'd say this during working hours, but, why don't you go play tennis. Burn some of that excess energy off." Edith looked weary.

"You and I must be on the same wavelength, Edith. I have a lesson at Mill Creek today with one of the pros who is boinking almost every female at the club. He has to know something."

Edith suddenly got serious. "We need a break in this story, Charlie. If you think this pro knows something, I want you to boink him, too."

"Edith, I may do some crazy things, but I am discriminate when it comes to men and I will not be a Bugle boinker. I'm a mother for goodness sakes."

"Think of yourself as a modern day Mata Hari," Edith said.

"This conversation is ridiculous," I replied.

"Jim Greco may be moving in a few weeks. He has a fantastic view of the Delaware River," Edith sniffed.

Edith and I locked eyes.

"You solve this case by the time he leaves and that office is yours."

Was she for real? A door, a window, a water view? With a newfound determination, I picked up my purse and headed out to Mill Creek.

I thought I heard Edith whisper to Inge: "Of course, Charlie may be in jail before Jim leaves."

When I walked into Mill Creek, the lobby was bustling, as usual. I saw Jazzy and her team sitting on the couch looking at an oversized photo album. I gave Cindee my credit card to pay for the lesson. I noticed some brochures with a group picture of Jazzy's team on the front.

"What's this?" I asked Cindee. I picked up a brochure.

"Collette asked if we could leave the brochures at the desk. They're collecting used cans of tennis balls and gently used racquets and tennis clothes and then they ship everything to this tennis school in Africa."

There was a big basket with the sign "used cans of tennis balls" and "gently used tennis clothes and racquets" for charity.

I read the front page of the brochure: "Mill Creek's Mood Swings sponsor tennis school in Malawi." "SERVING CHILDREN IN AFRICA'S MALAWI" There a team picture of the Mood Swings and then there were several smaller pictures of African children playing tennis and being taught by pros.

"Who would have thought? I'm impressed," I said to Cindee.

I wandered over to the couch. Several of the Mood Swing girls were looking at a photo album. "Hi!" I said.

"Hi, Charlie," said Collette.

"What are you looking at?" I asked.

"It's a photo album of the tennis camp in Malawi," Jazzy said.

"Look how cute Teremzi looks. The racquet is almost bigger than he is." said Maria Theresa. "Bless his soul."

"Who took the pictures? How did you get involved?" I asked.

"I took zah photos," said Collette.

"How did you hear about the charity," I asked.

"My husband, Claude, and I lived in Africa for awhile. He was Senior VP of Marketing there plus Asia and Latin America. We both saw so much poverty in Malawi that we came up with zah idea of starting a tennees camp. Claude asked his boss who met with the CEO of Tower Glenn, and voila, we now have a fully funded tennees camp with ten pros and a hundred students," Collette explained.

"If you have any old tennis clothes or balls, we're shipping out four boxes this Saturday," said Jazzy.

"Oh, I'll definitely look," I said. "And, I'm sure my boys have some old racquets I can give you."

"How's the investigation coming?" asked Jazzy.

"Unfortunately, the only suspects are me and my friend, Robin," I said.

"Oh, yeah, I read about that in the paper. She's a witch, right? And she gave you a magic potion or something," said Maria Theresa.

"She left a vial of oil on my desk to 'dress' the candle."

"What does 'dress' mean?" Collette asked.

"While the candle is burning you pour the oils over it and it enhances the intensity of the candle. Certain candles need to be lit on certain days and that gives them more power," I said. I could tell no one was really listening. If the subject wasn't gossip, food or cures for tennis elbow, no one cared.

Chad poked his head from the courts and called me. "Hi! I'm ready for you."

I followed Chad onto the court. We began with reflex volleys.

"Any new news?" asked Chad.

"You think if I knew something that no one else knew, I'd tell you?"

"Move your feet. Don't chop." Silence. "I didn't give Jazzy that hickey, Charlie."

"Well, gee, now I really respect you." I hit a high pop up directly at Chad's crotch. He expertly blocked it of course.

"Good hands," I said. Hoping he would interpret said comment as double entendre.

"What do you want to work on?" Chad asked.

"Serve."

"Let's see what you've got."

He pushed the ball cart to the end of the court and I followed him. I hit a few serves and he stopped me mid motion.

"I'm sure it's not been lost on you that you're drop dead gorgeous and that women probably tell you their innermost secrets all the time." Perhaps the timing of my saying this wasn't the most effective. My arms were still up in the air, statue-like, in the "W" position.

He whispered in my ear. His breath gave me the chills. "The strongest connection between the two poisonings is you."

I lowered my arms. "You know something."

"Seek and ye shall find," Chad said.

"Huh?" I said.

"Keep digging, don't give up. With all the circumstantial evidence, you are the easiest to convict."

"And you think I'm innocent?"

"Yeah, I do," Chad said with sincerity.

"Why, if I'm the strongest connection?"

"I, I just don't think you did it, that's all. Lots of people had access to the soup."

"Do you think Nora could have done it? She was there that day. That's what Jazzy thinks."

"Did you ever find out what kind of poison it was?" Chad asked.

"Well, the first poisoning was cyanide. The second poisoning was cyanide and some toxic oils that were taken from a vial on my desk and dumped in Plug's soup at the restaurant.

"Well, that narrows it down a bit," Chad said sarcastically. "You need to write down everyone who was both at the match and the restaurant. I do think the second poisoning is more damning for you."

"I know. First time, that was simply an accident with the soup that anyone could have made. I reached for the jar of ground coriander, and grabbed the cyanide by mistake."

"Lots of people do that," Chad agreed.

"I know. But, the second time at the restaurant? Even though I had no physical contact with her soup, I'm being blamed."

"Probable cause."

"That's just what the police said," I nodded.

We moved up to the net and did reflex volleys.

"You should also ask yourself what was the connection between the two women who were poisoned."

"That's just what the police asked," I said.

Chad was much better at talking and playing than I was.

"Racquet out in front, lead with the butt handle…like a hammer…." He demonstrated the "v" type movement.

We volleyed a bit more.

"Too much swing. If you can't see the racquet out in front when you hit the volley, then you're taking too much backswing."

"The obvious connection is that they were tennis partners. This guy at work thinks I killed Grace because she didn't play me at Districts last summer. Isn't that stupid?" I asked incredulously.

"Who's the guy?"

"Roscoe Minsk."

Chad gave me a funny look. I laughed.

"I know. With a name like that you'd think he'd be next on my list…just so I wouldn't have to say the name anymore."

"Next on your list?" Chad asked.

"You know I was being facetious."

"Facetious or Freudian…which is it?"

The basket was empty. I started picking up the balls with a hopper.

"Although Freud did say, 'Many a true word is said in jest,' Freud was not hounded through high school by Roscoe. After I turned him down for the prom, he made my life miserable. He maligned me in the school paper, spread nasty rumors about me, and purposely left out my picture in the graduation yearbook. Isn't that mean and immature?" I could feel my face flush.

Chad laughed. "I can see he still gets you hot and bothered. You're face is bright red."

"Thanks for the lesson," I walked off the court feeling annoyed.

When I keyed into my house, I was in shock. I had forgotten how much packing and labeling I still needed to do. The ironing table was set up in front of the TV, with clothes piled on top of it and strewn about all over the floor. Trunks for camp were being picked up tomorrow morning. First things first, I poured myself a glass of wine and went upstairs to check my e-mail.

"Line-up for match tomorrow", I saw in the subject line. I clicked on it. Good, I was playing with Savannah. Junk, junk, junk, delete, delete, delete. Oh, crap, another jewelry party. The subject line said "Jewelry of the Sea." This one was given by Colette. "Come see exclusive French imported bracelets, necklaces and earrings with unique semi-precious stones and European styling." There was always the pressure to buy at these parties. And, the jewelry was always 'stone' ugly and over-priced. The worst were the "Happy Cook" parties. Cheap cookware and cheesy hors d'ouerves. Oh no. It was a combination Jewelry/Happy Chef party. Colette and Jazzy were doing it together.

"What can I bring?" I saw myself typing. It was an unwritten rule in the tennis world that you always attend these parties.

"Just yourself. Please, please, don't bring anything!" was the quick response from Jazzy.

That's odd, I thought. I took a big gulp of wine. "Oh, I get it. Everyone's scared to eat anything I make now," I said aloud. Hmmf!

"I'm not scared. I'll eat anything, I'm starved!"

Who was that?! The noise was coming from my closet. My heart stopped beating. I looked for something to pick up. I lifted my tennis ball paperweight, swiveled around in my chair, took aim and...I didn't see anyone.

"You stay right there! I'm, I'm going to call the police!" I screamed.

"Charlie, stop!"

The voice sounded familiar. I saw a head peek out of my closet. It was Bradley.

I breathed a huge sigh of relief. "Bradley, what are you doing here?"

"The Mafia is after me."

"And, you're hiding out, here? I have kids Bradley, you can't stay here."

"I saw the trunks, your kids are leaving Monday for the summer."

"I'm not going to endanger my children," I said angrily. "You need to leave!"

"Look who's talking. You're an alleged murderer."

He had me. I was actually glad that Marshall had the boys till Monday. I was still getting threatening emails and texts. We had made arrangements for him to bring the boys to a restaurant parking lot Monday morning at 8:00 AM, on his way to work. I would take them to breakfast then bring them to the high school where camp busses were leaving at 9:00 AM. I was already homesick for them.

"I'm a great ironer, let me help. After I get something to eat, of course."

I looked at the casts on both his legs and the cast on his left arm. It was as if Bradley was reading my mind.

"No worries, I'm right handed," Bradley said swinging his right arm.

"How did you escape from the hospital? Actually, how did you physically walk down the hallway of the hospital?"

"I have friends in high places," Bradley said.

I wasn't in the mood to smile.

"That was a joke."

I helped Bradley down the steps and whipped up a quick shrimp scampi for dinner.

"Do you have parmesan cheese?" he asked.

I handed him a plastic container, with freshly grated Parmesan cheese.

"No, the real stuff."

"This is the real stuff," I said.

"No, no, do you have a block of parmesan cheese and a grater."

"Bradley, I have two kids who will give me about 15 minutes for a sit down dinner. Manually grating Parmesan cheese every time they want cheese is not gonna happen. This Parmesan cheese is from a high-falutin' gourmet store. They grate the cheese there and put it in these containers."

"Mmmm, ok. I guess I'll use it. Do you have any fresh, chopped parsley?"

"I don't have time for this." I poured myself a second glass of wine. "The good news is, after 2 glasses of wine, I won't care whatever you ask for."

I went to the living room, plugged in the iron and went to work. Bradley actually turned out to be very helpful. He somehow situated himself on the floor, and folded and packed as I handed him labeled socks, underwear, shirts, shorts, sweats, blankets, flashlights, and toiletries.

At 11:00 we were finished. And, so were two bottles of wine. I drank my requisite two glasses and Bradley polished off the rest. He fell asleep on the floor. I lifted him on the couch, put a pillow under his head and covered him with a quilt.

I stared at Bradley.   What was going on?   My life was becoming more and more complicated..

CHAPTER 10

I met my boys at "BATTER UP" the next morning. It was a baseball themed pancake house and my boys' favorite breakfast place. I met Marshall in the parking lot and we tried to act civil.

"How was jail?" asked Marshall.

So much for civil. I gave Marshall a look, incredulous that he brought up my infamous night in front of the kids.

"Not as much fun as those 'gentleman' (I made quote marks with my fingers) clubs that your wife dances in," I smiled sweetly. "Great role model for the kids."

I quickly ushered them into the restaurant. It was a very kitschy inside. Food was served on a large tray shaped like a catcher's mitt, drinks came in hollowed out baseballs, and the walls were decorated with posters of famous players and various baseball paraphernalia. I had the home run: three banana pancakes with blueberry syrup, turkey sausage and a large coffee. Nothing like mass quantities of food to assuage my nerves. Jake had a Grand Slam: four chocolate chip pancakes, bacon, and a large milk. And, Josh had the no-hitter: Large cheese omelet, home fries, two pieces of toast and a large orange juice.

"Thanks for taking us here," said Josh. "Yeah, thanks, Mom," Jake said.

"I'm gonna miss you guys." I squeezed their hands. "We're gonna miss you, too," said the boys together.

"So, I just wanted to tell you that we have a guest staying the night, but please don't tell Dad. It's one of my co-workers: Bradley.

"Why is he staying at our house? Doesn't he have his own house?" Josh asked.

"Yes, he has his own house, but, um, he had an argument and he needed a place to clear his head," I said. This was not a convincing lie. I was sure I had a Pinocchio nose by now.

"Is Bradley your new boyfriend?" asked Jake.

"No, oh no, not my boyfriend. He's just a friend from work that I'm helping out."

"Do you mind if I sit down?" Alex asked.

"Well, well, well, what happened to you? Thanks for all your help when I was in…(I looked at my boys)…you know. If it wasn't for my editor, I'd probably still be there."

"Nothing I could have done. I work for the DA, remember? My job is to put you in…(he looked at my boys)…you know. But, I do have some interesting news. Analysis was done on the soup that Plug ate. And, although the soup did contain oils from the vial taken from your desk, it also had Cyanide in it."

"The same poison that was in the soup that Grace ate," I said.

"What does that mean, Mom?" Jake asked.

"It means the same person was involved in both poisonings and was trying to frame your mom by using the vial on her desk at work," Alex said.

I looked at Alex as he spoke. Amazing how he had changed from the barking cop when I first met him to this mellow charmer. And, he smelled good, too. He had that fresh soap smell, like he just got out of the shower. His brown hair was wet and slicked back and his blue eyes were intense and sparkled.

"How's your girlfriend?" Damn! Why did I say that? Because I had a bad habit of saying what I was thinking, that's why

"She's in Texas for a week on a conference."

The boys whispered something to each other and smiled.

"What are you up to now?" he asked.

"After breakfast, I'm taking the boys to the bus stop for camp. The buses are meeting at the high school."

"Do you need help?" Alex asked.

"Well, I could probably handle everything," I said.

"Do you want company?"

I felt two feet kick each of my shins under the table.

"Ow! Yes, I guess I do want company." I glared at the boys.

I paid the check and Alex followed us to the High School. The parking lot was really crowded. Alex helped me load the busses with the boys' luggage. As independent as I was, it was nice having a man around. I gave both boys a huge hug, reminded them to write and cried when the buses pulled away. Instinctively, Alex put his arms around me. And, then we kissed. We must have kissed for a long time, because by the time we stopped, the busses had disappeared and the parking lot was empty.

"This is bad, really bad," Alex said. "I'm supposed to be investigating you."

"Well, let's go back to my place and continue the investigation," I said as I kissed him again.

"It's just that you're so cute, funny and…and…" Alex sighed.

"And?"

"Vulnerable. You're in a lot of trouble. There's a part of me that wants to save you. Do you have a lawyer yet, by the way?"

"No."

"Charlie, you need a lawyer."

"If I had a lawyer, the lawyer would tell me to stay away from you. What time is it, by the way? I have a funeral to go to."

"It's 11:30. I'm so sorry. Who passed away?"

"Bucky Birnbaum." Alex just stared at me. "He was a hamster…a Jewish hamster. This is the other (I made quote marks) hot story Edith has me covering. Bucky was allegedly poisoned at an Elementary school. She wants me to find out who poisoned Bucky."

"He didn't have any of your soup, did he?"

"Ha, ha."

We picked up the conversation in my car.

"What have you got so far?" Alex looked genuinely interested.

"A bunch of 6th graders who are afraid to talk, a secretary that really wants to talk, and a principal who won't talk. I can't tell if Principal Paul knows who did it or if he just doesn't want scandal."

"How do you know Bucky was poisoned?" Alex asked.

"Everyone is assuming he was poisoned. He died suddenly at school and the family wanted an autopsy done. Bucky was a cherished family pet. Still waiting for a detailed analysis."

"Speaking of analysis, I do have one new piece of information. More lab results came back from the soup you made at the tennis club and not only was their cyanide in there, they found several poisonous mushrooms chopped in with the soup."

"That's fantastic news!" I smiled.

"It is?"

"Sure. I made chicken tortilla soup. Everyone knows that you don't put mushrooms in with that type of soup."

"On the other hand, you're a food critic. Someone with your knowledge of food would know what type of mushroom you would use to poison someone."

"Oh, Alex. Anyone with a computer would know what types of mushrooms are poisonous. Clearly the person who did it, wanted to make it look like I did it. By putting a poisoned food in the soup. But, where would someone find poisoned mushrooms? I wouldn't know where to start looking for that."

"Okay. So how do you explain the toxic oils found in Lilly Wirthenheim's soup?" Alex asked. "It doesn't make any sense. Why not just the cyanide?"

"Whoever is doing this is obviously preoccupied with poison: cyanide, oils and now mushrooms."

"I bet the killer is thinking he can cover his tracks better by muddying up the waters with different poisonous elements."

"Alex, I'm so confused, and scared. I need to clear myself before the kids come home from camp. Suppose I can't go to Visiting Day?" I looked at my watch. "I've got to go to the funeral and I'm sure you've got to go to work."

"Uh, yeah. I'm late," Alex said, suddenly looking preoccupied. "Let's talk this afternoon."

I was 20 minutes late when I pulled into The Roosevelt cemetery. Color-coded wooden arrows indicated different funerals. Bucky's was blue. I followed blue arrows until it led me to plot site D. There were only about 10 people there, so it would be hard for me to blend in with the crowd. I put on my Audrey Hepburn scarf and glasses. I was wearing a sleeveless black shirt, and a black skirt cinched with a black Patent leather belt. Black pumps finished the outfit. Thankfully, the funeral had already started. As unobtrusively as I could, I inched my way to the tent where everyone was standing. Unfortunately, my pumps weren't cooperating. Darn! They were digging into the ground as I walked. It had rained last night.

I stood just inside the tent. The coffin was doll-sized. I felt an inappropriate giggle coming on. I took out a tissue and sneezed as I laughed. Everyone turned and I managed to turn a giggle-sneeze into a very respectable teary-bawl. A woman standing next to me put her arms around me and whispered, "Just let it out. Bucky would want that. He had more emotion in his tiny furry body than most people I know." Uh oh. I took out another tissue. Laugh-laugh coming. Thankfully, the Rabbi starting talking.

"Before I say the final blessing, would anyone like to share their memories of Bucky?" The Rabbi surveyed the group. "Anyone?" A little boy raised his hand. "Justin? What would you like to share about Bucky?"

"My mom always made me clean up his poop in the cage and feed him because she was always too busy."

The father and mother looked at each other. Standing from behind, I couldn't get a good look at their expressions. I'm sure they weren't happy. "He was your pet, Justin, it was your responsibility," said the mom.

And then Justin cried. He cried and he cried. He buried his head in his hands and sat on the grass. The dad knelt down and tried to comfort him. The mom just stared. After Justin calmed down, the Rabbi recited the Mourner's Kaddish. Everyone, including myself, took turns shoveling dirt onto the coffin. I kept my head down, still trying to stay incognito.

I looked at the nameplates of the four other Birnbaum's buried there as I shoveled dirt on the tiny coffin. I looked at the small hole waiting for the small coffin. And then, I started crying. Memories of my mother and father started flooding through my mind. They had both died so young. My mother was my best friend. By the time I was 28, I had lost both my parents and I had no siblings. Bucky was only a hamster, but death was death. It was final. Robin believed in life after death, and so did my mother. I hoped she was right. The thought of never seeing my mother again was too much to bare. I don't know why I came. What did I hope to learn at Bucky's funeral? I was depressed when I came and more depressed leaving.

By the time I got to my car, my heels were thoroughly gunked up. I took them off, turned on the ignition, the air conditioning and then saw a fist pound on my window. It was the secretary from Langhorne Elementary. How could I have missed her at the funeral?

"Can I get in?" she asked urgently.

I unlocked the passenger side.

"Can we go somewhere?" she asked.

I looked around the cemetery. I weaved my way behind the administration building.

"What's this all about?" I asked.

"Have you found out anything more about Bucky? Did you call the animal hospital?"

"Unfortunately, not yet. I have a lot on my plate right now." Yeah, like clearing myself of murder

"I wanted you to know that I found two of these capsules yesterday in the classroom where Bucky's cage was kept. I was helping a maintenance man move a cabinet out into the hallway. We were replacing it with a new one. Anyway, I saw these two capsules. And, I thought it was odd to see capsules in a children's classroom. Medication is only given out and taken in the nurse's office.

"They could have been the teacher's." I examined the two capsules.

"I also thought you should know that Paul….the principal is having an affair with Justin's mother, Andrea. That's why he got a little crazy when you started asking questions. He told you the hamster was his. But, I guess now you know it was the Birnbaum family's. He wasn't thinking straight. I think he feels so guilt-ridden because he's cheating on his wife."

"I still don't have a motive about who or why anyone would want to kill a hamster. Anything else?"

"The only other thing I can think of is that the kids took turns each week feeding the hamster."

"How do you know this?

"I spoke to Joanne Gayle. She's the teacher of that class."

"Whose week was it to feed Bucky?"

"I don't know. I didn't ask. Just that one of the kids bought in a bottle of vitamins that he said were "Hamster" vitamins. Joanne looked at the bottle. It seemed okay. Hamsters eat people food and she thought there was no harm in giving the hamster vitamins. So, she told Joey it was okay." The secretary started to cry. "The kid gave Bucky one of the vitamins and Bucky started hyperventilating and then he just stopped breathing. Joanne feels awful. She said that she's the adult and she should never have let this happen."

"What happened to the bottle?"

"Joanne said she panicked. She took the bottle and threw it out in a trashcan in the cafeteria."

"Can I keep these?" I asked.

"Yes."

"Are there more?"

"It's possible that there may be a stray capsule hiding out somewhere in class. But, these two are all that I found."

"Just curious, why didn't you give these to the police? Why are you telling me?"

"Because you're a reporter for a newspaper. It's your job to get to the bottom of this. I don't trust the police to take the death of a hamster seriously. I don't know why, but I trust you."

"What's your name again?"

"Julie Quinn."

"Irish?" I asked.

"Half," said Julie

"Maybe that's why you trust me. I'm half Irish also. Father's side."

I drove Julie back to her car. Everyone at the funeral was gone.

"Good luck. I hope you catch the bad guy! Poor, little Bucky." Julie got out of my car and waved good-bye.

I looked at the clock. I was supposed to play a match at 1:00. I don't think I could concentrate. I picked up my cell and called Elaine.

"Elaine? Hi, it's Charlie. Can you get a sub today? I can't play. No, I'm not in jail. No, I didn't kill anyone else. I'm telling you the truth, I haven't killed anyone today...or any day. (beat) You're my teammate, right? Well, you're acting very accusatory. Oh, all right, I'll play!" I clicked off my cell and mimicked Elaine's whine: "Well, if you're not in jail you have to play."

My cell rang again. It was Edith.

"Hi Edith. I'm just leaving the funeral now. I'm going to write up a report when I get back. But, I, uh, thought it would be a good idea to play with, I, um, mean interview some of the tennis girls who were there when Grace died." It seemed like I was lying a lot lately.

I dialed my house. "Bradley? No, I don't know what's for dinner yet. Yes, it is good news you can move your left arm and your right leg. But, the reason why I called is that I ran into the secretary from Langhorne Elementary at Bucky's funeral today. She gave me two capsules that she found in the class where Bucky was kept. They're grey. Yeah, they have some markings. They're about an inch long. Really? Oh, no. Well, I'll be home later and I'll show you. Knowing you, you're right. Bye." Annoying, but right.

CHAPTER 11

Next stop was Mercer County Park. I would change in the bathroom there. We were playing "Got Balls?" Their team drills with Chad and he was great with strategy. I speed-dialed Jen. Thank goodness for Bluetooth, as I was driving in New Jersey, land of obnoxious cops.

"Hey Jen, it's me. Have you heard anything useful on the "Got Balls?"

"Well, you know they'll do anything to make it to Districts this year, so you know they'll stack. What court are you playing?"

"Either 1 or 2." I said.

"Well, if you play 1, you're going to be playing their 3 and if you play 2, you'll be playing their 1. And, you know they drill with Chad. He's great with strategy. He teaches over-loading and ball-side. High overheads go straight at the net person and they're going to play middle a lot."

"I know; they're a good team. And, they're out to prove something."

"You and Savannah will be fine," Jen said.

"I know. Our big strategy is that we're going to charm them to death. Savannah's so darn nice. It's disarming how nice she is." We both laughed, because we both knew that her Southern charm was deadly. "I'll see you there, I'm going to watch your match," said Jen.

When I arrived at Mercer, I saw my team warming up on the courts. I saw Chad talking to the team we were playing. I picked up my tennis bag and backpack and ran to the bathroom to change. Savannah was crying at the sink.

"Savannah, what's wrong?" I asked.

"It's the pressure. Ah can't stand it anymore."

"To win?"

"Yeah."

"You've played USTA forever. What else is going on?"

"Honey, everyone's talkin' about you. It's ugly. They think you did it, and they want to kick you off the team. Ah didn't want to tell you. But, it's gettin' to me."

"What about Jen?"

"Well, she didn't come to your defense when we had a team meetin'."

"You had a team meetin' without me?" I mimicked her Southern accent.

Savannah laughed.

"Let's go out there and cream our opponents and then I'll decide what to do."

I handed Savannah a tissue.

"Thanks for being honest with me. So, what do you think? Do you think I did it?"

"You know what, ah was brought up in the deep South. Ah saw a lot of horrible things growing up. There was a lot of prejudice. But, my parents taught me that pre-judging people is ignorant and wrong. I'm 5 foot 10 and gay, Charlie. I know people talk about me and look at me funny. I know the only reason ahm on this team is because I'm a 4.0 who should be a 4.5. From where ah stand, I have no room to judge you."

"I guess I'm guilty of prejudice, too. I wanted to play with you before I even knew you because you were gay and from the South. Isn't that weird? I just knew you'd be a fun person to play with and a strong tennis player."

"And?"

"And, I was right.

Savannah and I left the bathroom, arm in arm. Somehow, I was always letting myself get disappointed by these tennis girls. I thought Jen was my friend, and that really hurt. I usually made myself feel better by repeating the mantra, "I'm just playing USTA for the exercise and camaraderie." Well, I needed to edit the mantra. Obviously, there was no camaraderie.

"Charlie, thank goodness you're here," screamed Elaine. You and Savannah are on court 2. You're playing Cecilia Chen and Ruby Taylor. Here are your balls. Komen tie-break if you go to three sets."

They did put 1 on 2. Jen was right. Cecilia was all about the net and angled everything. She was steady and crafty. Ruby was a retriever and hung out on the baseline, setting her partner up. Our strategy was to take Ruby out of her comfort zone and short shot her to bring her to net, then lob over her and we would take over the net. Keep everything away from Cecilia and keep them off balanced. I was good at that.

Our match was certainly a battle. There was intense strategy and craftiness on both sides. We won the first set 6-3. Ruby and Cecilia changed their strategy. They both started chipping and charging, after a service return, trying to put pressure on our returns. We countered that with returning down the middle, which caused confusion on their side. Ruby wasn't used to coming in. We also started serving and volleying and playing "I formation" when either of us served. Ruby and Cecilia started making return errors and also started double-faulting more. We won the second set 6-2.

Savannah and I shook hands with our opponents. I was glad it was a friendly match and there wasn't any on-court drama. Elaine was all smiles. Jen, Barb, and Devon clapped wildly when we stepped off the court.

"We just won the match! We needed your court," said Devon.

"Do either of you want a Tylenol...with Codeine?" asked Barb. "It's easy to get a migraine in this heat."

"No thanks, Barb," we both said.

"Are you both going to Jazzy's 'Happy Chef' party tonight?" asked Elaine

"Hard to believe she invited me. She told me not to bring anything in an email. But, I can't come empty handed." Uh, and, do I really want to hang out with all of you tonight?

"Just bring something sealed," said Devon. "Like chips and a jar of salsa."

"I'm surprised she invited our team," said Maryellen. "I thought they all hated us."

"They do hate us. It's all about the sales. Jazzy gets free 'Happy Chef' stuff, depending how much she sells," said Elaine.

"Just what I need, another cheap vegetable peeler," said Jen. She smiled at me but I was expressionless.

"I need to run," I said.

"Me, too. Bye y'all," said Savannah.

"Hey, Charlie, can I talk to you?" asked Jen.

"Not now, I have to go."

I ran to my car, turned the air on and headed home. It was a long and emotional day. I missed my kids. My cell phone beeped. It was a text from Edith. STAFF MEETING AT 4:00! Cripes! It was 3:15 and I was covered in sunscreen and sweat. I was supposed to be on the job, investigating two crimes and Edith would be furious when she sees me and finds out I don't have any new information. I was 25 minutes from Mill Creek, but that was in the opposite direction of work. I got out of the car and looked around. Maybe there was a public shower at the park?

"Hey!" Chad called from across the parking lot.

"Hi, Chad!

"Nice match against Ruby and Cecilia. You both played smart."

"Thanks," I said.

"You look worried. What's wrong?"

"I have a staff meeting at 4:00. I don't have enough time to go home and shower. And if I show up like this, I'll be fired."

"Playing USTA matches during working hours isn't in your job description?"

"I'm too panicked to talk. My editor is terrifying…and that's when I'm properly dressed."

"You're in luck. I live 5 minutes from here, and you're welcome to use my shower."

"I'm sure."

"You don't trust me…or is it that you don't trust you?"

I don't trust me…okay? The entire female population of the whole world would jump at this invitation…so why was I hesitating? I was desperate to be clean, but somehow I could see an additional complication creeping into my life.

"I'm leaving now. Maybe there's a shower in the public restroom down the hill," Chad said.

Public restroom shower…if there even was one…or gorgeous tennis pro shower. Why was I even weighing the two options?

"Okay! I'll take you up on your offer."

"Oh, thank you. Thank you!" Chad did a subservient bow.

I followed Chad to a very upscale townhouse complex. We parked next to each other. I grabbed my tennis bag from my trunk. Thankfully, I always carried a clean set of clothes. I nervously followed him into his house. The furniture was also upscale, but sparse.

"The bathroom is up the steps to the left. Shall I pour you a glass of wine to help you prepare for your meeting?"

Before I could say no, Chad poured me a glass of wine. "Drink it as you climb the steps. No time to waste."

If he weren't sleeping with everything that wasn't nailed down at the club, this guy would be a dream. I took the glass of wine from him and drank as I made my way up the stairs. Just as I peeled off my clothes, I heard a knock. I knew it. What a low-life.

"What?" I yelled at the closed door.

"You forgot your bag," I heard back.

I cracked the door and Chad handed me my bag and another glass of wine. I locked the door again. I was prejudging him, just the way I was being prejudged by all the tennis girls. I was no better than they were. I took a few sips of the second glass of wine.

After my shower, I was not only clean, but drunk. Perfect. Just the way I needed to be for a staff meeting with Edith. I walked down the stairs, unsteady, but smiling.

"Much better. You don't look tense anymore," Chad said grinning.

"Now all I have to worry about is being able to drive and not throwing up at the meeting. All kidding aside, thank you so much. You were a life-saver."

I gave Chad a hug. He opened the door for me. "Anytime." His cell phone rang. "I've got to get this. Good luck!" And he closed the door.

His mail had spilled out of his mailbox, onto the ground. I gathered it up and was about to knock on his door, but decided that I didn't want to bother him. I stuffed it back into his mailbox, and then noticed a Fed-Ex. It had a French return address and was from a woman, Sabine Gadal. I could not make out the address, just the city, Lyon, France. Man, this guy does get around. My cell phone beeped. I jumped. It was from Robin. "Don't forget 4:00 meeting. Edith in unworldly bad mood today." I text back, "Will be there. I am drunk. Impervious to anything right now." Robin texted back, "????"

I pulled into the Bucks Bugle parking lot right at 4:00. Still feeling a bit tipsy, I zigzagged to the front door and stumbled into the building. Pull yourself together, I said to myself. You can do this. I looked left than right. Where was the conference room? We only had one…right? Somehow, I steered myself in the right direction, I did a double take when I saw Prudence gathering some papers at her desk…in a cubicle!

"Pudence? Izzat you?" I slurred.

"I'm in the doghouse, Charlie. When Edith found out I was auditioning to be YNOT's weather girl and didn't let her know, she moved me out of my office and into this cubicle. It's awful. No more window view. I can't see when it's raining or snowing or blowing. I used to watch the wind move leaves for hours."

"For hours?"

"Weather is a small department. Not a lot to do. I mostly make up the weather column. That's the beauty of doing weather. No one expects the weather person to be right, so you're never wrong."

"Except when Edith whrains on your paaarrade," I tried.

"What? Charlie, are you on some medication?"

"I'm high on life, Pru. Come on!" I motioned her to follow me, still not sure where I was going.

Prudence poured two cups of coffee and handed me both. "Drink these, quick! We're late and you're either drunk or tripping on acid!" Prudence held open the conference door for me.

"Well, well, look what the cat dragged in," Edith glared at us. "I must apologize for making this meeting an inconvenient time for both of you. I know that your schedules are much more important than all of ours." Edith pulled out her plastic cigarette holder from the pocket of her ruffled blouse, stuck it in her mouth and bit down on it. Even in my drunken stupor I could see she was seething with anger.

I took a quick head count around the conference table: Wally, Robin, Stanley, Inge, Roscoe, and Jim. What did Jim do again? He didn't have a column, yet he was always on his computer typing away. What was he working on, his memoirs?

"Okay, now that we're all here," Edith stared at me and Prudence, "I want to hear what everyone's got. We go to print at 1:00 AM sharp. Robin!"

Robin hated being called on first. She opened her mouth but nothing came out. Like me, she was petrified of Edith."

"Tubing for Ten?" asked Robin hopefully.

"Dollars or people?" asked Edith.

"Dollars and people. A dollar a person. You bring your own tube and your own food. There's just a $1.00 water fee. 'Tubing for $10!" said Robin, hoping if she said it again with extra enthusiasm that Edith would go for it.

"We did the dollar water thing last year, 2nd week of June. Next idea," sniffed Edith.

Robin looked panicked. There was no next idea.

"Pennies in Peddlers!" I blurted out. All heads turned to me. Okay, one of the few good things about being me, was that I happened to be a fantastic liar. And, I was a quick liar, too. "Robin wasn't sure that you would like the Peddler's Village idea, so she was hesitant," I slurred. "She was hesitant," I repeated, "to tell you."

"'Pennies in Peddler' Edith motioned with her hands, like it was the star attraction on a Ziegfield Follies billboard. "I like the sound of that!" Said Edith. She had taken her plastic cigarette holder from her mouth and was now scratching her ear with it. And then she put the holder back in her mouth. Eww! Was I just imagining this? I might have been. Everything in the room started swirling around, in a Salvadore Dali meets Picasso sort of way. I started visualizing how Salvadore and Picasso would paint Edith's ear and the cigarette holder. What a fantastic collaboration that would be. All of a sudden I felt someone poking my back.

"Charlie! Charlie!" I heard Edith. My head had fallen onto the conference table. "Someone prop up, Charlie!" shouted Edith. "You were saying, Charlie, 'Pennies in Peddlers.'"

"Uh, yeah. In celebration of July 4th, there's a Patriotic Parade down Main Street, a Contemporary Crafts Contest, and free face painting for the kids, courtesy of Miss Fancy Paints. 'A free day, just pennies away.'"

Robin mouthed "Thank you," to me.

"Robin, I need a write up on "Pennies" by six o'clock sharp. Prudence, your restaurant write-up…what have you got?"

I took a look at Prudence. Prudence got nothin'. She looked helpless, too. She looked at me with pleading eyes. Man, if only I could get paid for lying.

"Prudence, I'm sure Edith would like your "Frolicking in Fondue" piece," I urged.

"I like it already," said Roscoe. "Sounds kinky."

"Gee, Charlie, "The Iceman Cometh," she giggled. "I'm afraid sometimes I get a brain-freeze with public speaking. Do you think you could talk about that idea for me?"

I didn't have the heart to correct Prudence and say that The Iceman Cometh" had nothing literally to do with ice. It was a Eugene O'Neil play about prostitutes and dead-end alcoholics. Prudence and her weather clichés, geez. But, Prudence did get me two cups of coffee. Here goes:

"Fondue for You" has taken a page from the Moroccan style of eating and encourages the diner to eat everything with their fingers. From lamb kabobs to pineapple pieces, cup-sized kettles are filled with a mélange of melted Milky Ways and gooey Gouda, to dip those cube-sized morsels in. Fondue for two? No skewers for you!" I should come drunk to meetings more often. That was good, very good.

"I am impressed, Prudence." Now Edith was tapping the cigarette holder on the table. "And even more impressed how Charlie has become the spokesperson for all my columnists. Let's see, who haven't we heard from?"

"Jim!" I said.

Jim looked startled. Edith never called on Jim, and Jim never spoke at meetings, or to anyone. He gave Edith a "What's up with this?" look. Edith responded by tapping the cigarette holder on her teeth. Lordy, is there anywhere that holder hasn't been…or wants to go? I quietly chuckled at my joke.

"Is there something funny you'd like to share with us, Charlie?" Asked Edith.

"Well, I was just wondering why Jim never had to speak at these meetings. And, also, why he got the corner office. I mean, what does Jim actually do?"

Everyone gasped around the table. Everyone but Jim, that is. Jim looked insulted. He gathered his papers.

"I'm, I'm sorry Jim," Edith said.

As Jim opened the conference door, he gave me a parting dirty look.

"I hope you're satisfied, Charlie. Jim has been thinking of taking a job in Altoona. I hope this didn't put him over the edge. The Bugle wouldn't be the same without him. Edith thought about this for a few seconds. "Charlie!"

My heart jumped.

"Any progress on the hamster story…and your story?"

I received smug smirks from Roscoe and Inge.

"I think Bucky ate some pills by mistake. Hamsters eat practically anything. The kids thought they were feeding Bucky a vitamin, but it obviously died from whatever that pill was. It was a terrible accident."

"So, the Peanut Chew wasn't poisoned?"

"Without an autopsy, I can't be 100% sure about anything," I said.

"I thought there was going to be an autopsy," Edith pressed.

"Of a hamster?" Roscoe was incredulous. He and Inge burst out laughing.

"Roscoe, Inge, if you two don't behave, I'm going to separate you and sit you both in the corner. Charlie, continue."

"I, I haven't found out about the autopsy yet." My palms were sweating. "I'm not even sure if there was one. But, I know I need to call the animal hospital and make sure. I did go to Bucky's funeral…"

Roscoe and Inge were rolling with laughter now.

"She vent to a hamster's funeral?" Inge laughed mockingly, in her thick German accent. "Did zay have a luncheon for za hamster aftervord?"

"Excuse me! Even a hamster has a right to a decent burial. The secretary of the school found some pills that had rolled under a cabinet. I'm going to show them to Bradley. He said he'll know more when he looks at the markings on the pills…(I put my hand over my mouth). That's all."

Everyone gasped again. No one knew what had happened to Bradley. He mysteriously had disappeared from the hospital. No one, but Edith, that is. She looked at me like I had just divulged the secrets to the atomic bomb to an unstable third world country.

"Bradley is staying with Charlie because the Mafia has a contract out on him. This has got to stay within these walls. Bradley's life depends on it."

"Why is he staying with Charlie?" asked Roscoe.

"By accident, he sat on the lap of a crime boss's girlfriend," said Edith.

"Okay. But, why with Charlie?" asked Roscoe again.

"We thought Charlie's house would be the least suspicious. But now...I don't know," sighed Edith.

"If her house is under surveillance, that's actually a good thing. It would mean there is a constant police presence," Robin said.

"My house isn't under surveillance. I am an 'alleged', murderer, remember?"

"What about that hot cop? I heard he's got you under surveillance!" Prudence smiled.

I glared at her. I just saved her ass. Why did she have to bring up Alex?

"It's his job to keep an eye on me."

"Any new news with lab analysis for the soups?" asked Edith.

"Cyanide in the Tortilla soup, cyanide in Lilly Werthenheim's soup at the restaurant and..."

"Cyanide in your purse!" accused Roscoe.

"What is there, a sale on Cyanide somewhere?" I mused.

"What's your next move, Charlie?" Edith asked.

"After the meeting, I'm going to sit down with Bradley and go over all the evidence and strategize what I should do next."

"Stanley?" Edith smiled sweetly.

Stanley pulled a pocket sized notepad, and a #2 pencil from his buttoned down shirt pocket. "As everyone knows, the paper's circulation has been steadily dropping at a rate of...." He pulls out a mini pocket calculator from the same pocket. He does several intricate calculations. "...2.8 percent. Down from..." Does several more calculations. "3.94 percent from last month. Which is....1.14 percent....down from....7 months ago."

I could see everyone's eyes glazing over at the table. But, somehow, Edith looked fascinated, and scarily, titillated. Her cheeks were flushed and she was beaming ear-to-ear.

"The paper needs additional advertising revenue to keep it afloat. I did meet with several nonprofits this month in my office, like the Serving Children in Malawi Foundation and the Ben Salem Bowler's Knocking Down Hunger Group who wanted to advertise charity events in our paper. But, unfortunately, they all wanted free advertising. And, it just wouldn't be fiscally responsible for me to give them free space."

"You have the paper's back, Stanley. And, we all appreciate your integrity and diligence."

But, her tone quickly changed.

"Roscoe, what have you got?" Edith said suddenly, pointing her cigarette holder at him.

"'Don't Bite your Cuticles…there's more firings in pharmaceuticals!' That's what I'm calling my piece about the nervous execs." Said Roscoe.

Edith frowned. "We'll have to work on the title. Go on."

Roscoe read his prepared piece: "With a 10 percent unemployment rate, people are buying more generics, delaying non-critical procedures, seeing their doctors less, because they're losing their health insurance. Consequently, to maximize profit, pharmaceutical companies are laying off senior and mid-level personnel, and hiring less experienced, younger people to do the same jobs. To make matters worse for the companies, there is a rise in counterfeiting brand name drugs."

I had to admit, what Roscoe wrote was good.

"Inge…international…what's going on?" asked Edith.

Suddenly my cell phone beeped. It was a reminder that at 6:00 I was receiving a camp call from both my kids. "Edith, unfortunately, I have to leave the meeting. I have a camp call from my kids in half an hour. I have to go home."

Edith gave a begrudging nod. Thank goodness she didn't lecture me. I gathered my papers, waved good-bye and left.

Alex met me in the parking lot. He grabbed me from behind. I squeaked.

"You scared me!"

"Sorry! I wanted to surprise you. Actually, I wanted to ask you. I saw you leaving Chad Cantwell's condo about two hours ago."

"So?"

"So, I thought you and I…"

"Alex, I like you, I really, really like you, but you have a girlfriend…that you're living with, and you're supposed to be investigating me. This is not a good situation. It's too complicated. I don't think it's a good time to get into a relationship. I have to clear myself and then hopefully, I can get custody of my kids again." I looked at my watch. "Nothing happened with Chad. He just let me use his shower."

"Let you use his shower?" Alex was seething.

"I have to go, I have a camp call from my kids. We can talk later on. Oh, wait a minute; I have a stupid party tonight. We can talk tomorrow." I kissed Alex on the cheek. He didn't know how hard this was for me, because I was still so attracted to him.

Since the first time I met Alex, he looked sad and deflated. "Oh, okay. We'll talk tomorrow. I'm going to follow you home, though, to make sure you're safe."

All of a sudden I heard a loud bang. Whatever it was, it shattered my rear windshield.

"Get down! That was a gun shot!" screamed Alex.

We waited for a minute but there weren't additional shots.

"I want you to drive with me! I can take you to a friend's house," Alex said.

"No, I need my car and I need to go home."

"Why are you being so stubborn? Somebody's trying to kill you."

"We'll talk about it tomorrow. My kids are calling in half an hour. I have to go!" Why didn't he understand that I needed to hear my children's voices? "The camp only lets you talk to your kids for a 15 minute scheduled call twice a summer. They're very strict."

I got in my car. There was no glass on the front seat. My foot was shaking as I pressed down on the break, releasing it. I saw Alex climb in his undercover cop car. The ride home was uneventful. Alex followed close behind.

After I pulled into my garage, I saw Alex drive away.

When I walked in the house, Bradley greeted me with a glass of wine and the aroma of a freshly baked apple pie. "I bake," he smiled.

"I can smell that," I said.

Just then the phone rang. I ran upstairs and closed my office door. I picked up the phone and put it on "speaker." "Mom?" "Hi, Jakie. How's camp?" "It's great! We're going to Dorney Park on Saturday, but I don't have enough money at the bank. I need you to send more." "How much?" "Can you send a hundred dollars?" "A hundred dollars?" "They said you need to wire the money so it gets here in time." "How's everything else?" "Good. I made a goal in soccer today. And, I got cooking for my elective." Cooking was the most popular elective because it was one of the only buildings in the camp with air-conditioning. We spoke for another 10 minutes. I kept my eye on the clock to make sure I got my full 15 minutes. "Do you want to speak with Josh, he's here." "I love you, Jake! Don't forget to write!" A few seconds later. "Hi, Mom!" said Josh cheerily. "Can you send more money?" "How much?" I asked weakly. "A thousand dollars. All the Lower seniors are going to Lake Placid, for five days." "Why didn't I remember this?" I asked. "I think because you said you were going to try and forget this, when I reminded you about the money in May," said Josh. Josh was my responsible one. He always kept a watchful eye on Jake at camp and at home. He worked hard at school, got good grades. But, an extra thousand dollars? For both kids, the 8 week camp was about $12,000. Enough for a cheap car and 3 months mortgage. Thank goodness Marshall made a good living as a dermatologist and I made a decent salary at the Bugle. We had agreed to split all camp expenses. But, maybe he would spring for the full thousand. "Okay, I'll make sure the camp bank gets the money in time. I love you and miss you!"

I checked my email. I clicked on a team email that Elaine sent. The subject line said: "High Strung is going to Districts!" "Congrats team! The Mood Swings lost yesterday, so we are the wildcard team and going to Districts! We have a two-hour mandatory practice tomorrow at 2:00 PM at the Mill Creek

Middle School. Anyone who doesn't go should not expect to play in the first Districts match. Except, Devon. Devon, thanks for letting me know you can't make it to practice. ☺" Give me a break, Devon the bully doesn't have to go to practice and she also gets a smiley face? She's a singles player who always wins, that's why.

Next, I clicked on the Evite reminder: There was a picture of a finger with a bow tied around it. "Don't forget, it's a night of fun, food and fabulousness at The Happy Chef party tonight at 7:00PM at Jazzy's." And then I clicked on who was coming which was everyone. About 50 girls would be there. What a nightmare and why am I going?

"Charlie! Charlie" screamed Bradley from downstairs.

"Coming!" I clicked on one more email from Mill Creek tennis club: "A gentle reminder that we are looking for gently used tennis clothes, balls and racquets to send to the 'Serving Children In Africa's Malawi' organization. As you know, the Mood Swing Team is a sponsor of this charity. Not only do the children learn how to play tennis, but the camp also provides three square meals a day and has an onsite swimming facility. Maria Theresa and Dal will be picking up the boxes of donated items on Saturday morning. And while you're here, jump in to one of our all-level drills starting at 8:00 AM and then challenge yourself in a Butt-Busters class at 10:00. ***Attention ladies….Chad will be teaching this class!"

"Charlie!"

"I'm coming, I'm coming!" Did I miss something, or was I married again?

I ran downstairs. "What is so urgent, Bradley?"

"I heard from one of my sources today. He's afraid that the mob may have found out I'm staying here."

"And, they wanted to let me know, that they know, by shooting out the rear windshield of my car. You need to leave."

I looked at Bradley. One leg was still in a cast and one arm had a splint. He was making progress, but still looked pathetic. The truth was, he was growing on me, like mold on a 6-month wedge of triple Brie. You knew if you scraped the mold off, you would likely still find a fine cheese, but its essence would still be the same: pungent and offensive.

He cut me a slice of pie. "Pie?"

"I'll have a piece when I come home. I have a Happy Chef/Jewels of the Nile party tonight. No matter how hard I try to stay away from these tennis ladies, they somehow find a way to draw me back into their claws."

"I don't get it. You're always bitching about them, saying how trivial and mean they are and then you go to their house for a party?"

"I'm a tennis masochist, I know. And they don't even trust me enough to bring anything."

"You want to bring this pie?"

"Thanks, but it's not sealed and they would never believe I didn't make it. But, there's something more important that I need to show you."

I unzipped the inside pocket of my purse and pulled out the two capsules given to me by the secretary at the funeral.

Bradley took a look at the capsules.

"Do you know what drug this is?

"I'd have to do some research on the markings."

"Do you think they could be cyanide pills?"

"No, these aren't cyanide pills." Bradley looked worried. He knew something else. But, I didn't have time to talk.

"I have to run, Bradley. I need to stop and get a bottle of wine."

CHAPTER 12

When I arrived at Jazzy's house, I was taken aback with how many cars there were. By the time I found parking, I was a block away. I realized I had forgotten to stop at the liquor store. I hated coming to the party empty-handed. I did remember that Jazzy had a wine cellar. She was always bragging that she was a wine connoisseur and she and her husband had a wine cellar and...and, what was I thinking? Break into her wine cellar and bring her a bottle of her own wine? It wouldn't do any harm to see if she had a walkout basement.

The gate to the backyard was open. I slipped through and saw the door to the basement. I tried it, but it was locked. I walked away and then heard some kids run out into the yard and head towards the gate. I hit behind a shrub. After they walked past the shrub I quickly tried the door again. It was open. I went in and saw several doors. Suddenly, I heard someone come downstairs. No time to hide.

"Hi Charlie!" said Jan.

"Hi Jan." I liked Jan and we sometimes played together. She was on the Net Gains.

"There's a million people upstairs. I was looking for a bathroom. Jazzy said there was one in her basement," Jan said.

"How's the party?" I asked. Drats! Now I couldn't steal a bottle of Jazzy's wine.

"It's okay. I always feel like I have to buy something at these parties. Great wine, though. They're doing a cooking demonstration in a few minutes." Jan frowned. "I'm so mad I brought wine. What a waste of money. Who knew Jazzy had a wine cellar?"

I did. "I guess I'll head upstairs," I sighed.

I surveyed the room, looking around for Jazzy. As I suspected, there were the usual cliques of girls factioned off around the room, each group being a different team. The 40-45 year-olds usually talked about elbow and knee injuries, and the various methods that cured them. Enjoy these years girls, because the 45-50 year-olds (my group), not only had the injuries to contend with, but now we also had the mystifying menopausal thing. It was like our bodies (and bladders) suddenly became possessed by an evil entity: we were happy, sad, hot, cold, crying, laughing, bitchy...bitchy. It was like we had become Linda Blair from the Exorcist overnight. I could probably tick off ten women who could use an exorcism before they walked onto the court. Well, an exorcism and a double martini. Speaking of alcohol....I stopped looking for Jazzy and started the search for the bar. I felt someone poking my back. It was Barb.

"Hey, Charlie."

"Hi Barb."

"Busy night, you can't believe how many pills I've doled out. I think everyone here must either be having a migraine or a nervous breakdown."

And, then it hit me. The conversation I had had with Chad about Barb a while ago. Barb seemed to have access to every drug known to man, and she was the one that helped me bring the crockpot in. It would have taken her two seconds to slip something in there. Also, she wasn't asked back on the Mood Swing's USTA team, either. Grace and Lilly really cleared the decks of players they thought weren't strong enough.

"Barb, how come you always have so many drugs?"

"My husband is head of marketing for Tower Glenn, and he brings home samples of everything. It really makes me feel good helping people that don't feel well."

Or, poisoning people that do feel well, I thought.

"I keep going over in my head, how someone, like us, would have access to cyanide?"

"Are you accusing me of something?"

"No, no."

"Hi, Barb! Long time," said Devon.

"Yeah, like this morning. Great win, today!"

"I know. Sara should really be 4.5. She got bumped, but appealed and they let her go down."

I quickly moved away and headed to the bar. Cindee poured me a glass before I could grab a bottle.

"A friendly face." I said.

"I try and stay neutral," smiled Cindee.

"Can I talk to you for a second…in private?"

Cindee and I walked into the study, just off the front door.

"Is there any truth to the rumor that Nora is trying to sabotage the club because she and Gary are getting a divorce and the club is in his name?" I asked.

"That she's just trying to be vengeful? I wouldn't put it past Nora. She has priced the clothes so high at the club that they're hardly selling. It's like she doesn't care anymore. Every time it rains we can't play on at two courts. We've had a leaky roof for at least 10 years," Cindee sighed.

"Why doesn't Gary hire someone to fix it? The club is in his name. You'd think he'd want the value to stay up."

"Neither one wants to sink any more money into the club. And, now with the poisoning, the travel teams are scared to have lunch at our club."

"Which is good for Nora."

"Are you implying that Nora put the poison in the soup as a final dagger to the club?" Cindee asked.

"She has motive and she had access."

"Aren't you a food critic? You're sounding more like a detective," Cindee said.

"Right now, I'm a petrified suspect. Can I ask you one more question?

Cindee nodded, finishing her wine in one gulp. She had a pile of peanuts in her other hand that she was popping in her mouth faster and faster as the conversation went on.

"What is the deal with Henry? I saw him in the kitchen cleaning dishes at the opening night of Sacre Bleu."

"Oh, Nora got him a job there. He needed some extra money. She knows the owner."

We both looked at each other. Henry would have had access to Lilly's soup.

"Listen, there's something I should tell you about Henry. But, you've got to keep it a secret."

I nodded.

"You know that Henry was a big-time stringer for a lot of famous tennis players on the tour. Well, he traveled all over he world and somehow he must have gotten into drug trafficking in the early 90's. He was in jail for about 5 years, until his lawyer got him out on a technicality."

"Henry was a drug mule? Wait a minute, I think I remember our paper doing a story about that years ago. But, I didn't think it was this Henry. He was represented by the same lawyer as the Giosa family. But, why would Nora hire an ex-con? It doesn't make sense."

"Maybe because he's a great stringer or, maybe he's blackmailing her. I don't know all the details, but I think he found out that Nora was cheating with a pro and threatened to tell Gary."

"An affair? But, she's so…"

"I know," shuddered Cindee. "It's enough to make your skin crawl. But, if Henry told Gary then he would have divorced Nora long ago and it would have affected the divorce settlement. She had no idea then that the club was solely in his name. And the club is on about 10 acres of land. She knew the club was worth a fortune."

"Why didn't Henry just ask Nora for a large sum of money and be done with it? How do you know all this?"

"I've heard them talking. I've picked up the phone by mistake many times over the years. I practically live at the club. You cannot tell anyone this, Charlie. I'll be fired if Nora finds out."

"I guess Henry wouldn't be too happy, either. When I picked up my racquet from him, when Grace died, he took a tennis string and knotted it tight, right in my face."

"You don't want to get Henry angry. That's why I'm always extra nice to him."

"But, I still don't understand why Henry would implicate himself in a murder just to do Nora a favor. It doesn't make sense. Why would he jeopardize going back to prison? To put cyanide in soup once, maybe twice because he feels like he still owes Nora? He knows she had an affair. So he actually, has something over Nora."

"It does seem like there is an evil delicate balance between those two. But, I think Nora has the trump card. You know how she met Gary, right?"

"Yeah, they were both on the tour," I said. That was common knowledge at the club.

"Well, I remember reading when the whole drug mule thing came out about Henry that he was a supplier to a lot of players on the tour. Nora told me that she personally saw Henry selling drugs at parties. She never came forward with this information when Henry was on trial. Henry was her stringer and Gary's stringer. Out of loyalty, she never said a thing. If she ever told the police this, he would be convicted for sure. I bet she's blackmailing Henry now."

"Wow! She does have the trump card. So either Henry helps her extract her revenge on Gary or she goes to the cops."

"Yeah. She's totally done with Gary. I can't tell you how many times she's said to me, 'He can have the damn club, but it won't be worth anything when he tries to sell it.'"

Cindee looked drained, but she was the only person who really knew what was going on at the club.

"One more question. What's the deal with Eddie? He always seems so manic to me. The way he's always trying to market himself and make more money by pushing his drills. It's getting old."

"Eddie is extremely competitive and really jealous of Chad. He was the top pro at the club until Chad was hired. I don't think Eddie would have any reason to have poisoned the soup, though. Unless...."

"Unless?"

"Unless he couldn't pay a loan back. Everyone knows that Eddie is into sports betting."

"Well, I do know that Eddie likes making $5.00 bets. He used to want to make $5.00 bets with all the tennis girls about who was going to win different matches, which team would go to districts, who was going to win the different Slams. It was endless and unseemly."

"About a week ago, I was having a coffee with Andi Miller at Jitters. We started talking about all the pros, and she told me that Eddie borrowed a lot of money from her and when she asked for it back because her husband was being laid off from his job, he said he didn't know when he could get it."

"How much money? Did she say?"

"Well, you know Andi's pretty rich. She hinted that it was over $100,000. But, wouldn't say the exact amount."

"Boy, maybe he poisoned the soup, hoping to kill her off, so he wouldn't have to pay her back. That is a shit-load amount of money."

Suddenly, we heard a bell being rung in the kitchen.

"Saved by the bell. I didn't think it was possible, but you've cleaned me out of gossip."

"I owe you, Cindee." I gave her a quick hug.

Jazzy was screaming. "Ladies, ladies, we are now going to learn how to make the best quiche you've ever tasted."

We walked back into the packed kitchen. Jazzy was hosting the party for Corrine Wallace. Corrine proceeded to show us how the Happy Chef tools were superior in rolling out dough, grating cheese, dicing onions, and sautéing broccoli. We were all given samples of quiche to try.

"Time for dessert, ladies!" said Jazzy. And then we heard an obnoxiously loud bicycle horn. "As a special treat the Snarky Clown Express will be delivering a Happy Chef birthday cake, while riding his unicycle."

Clown! Did I hear clown? My palms started to sweat, my breathing became shallow, and I could feel tears starting to roll down my face. Just the thought of seeing a clown in such close proximity…it was too scary. I needed to leave.

Snarky suddenly unicycled into the kitchen holding a cake in one hand and a horn in the other. My shirt was drenched and I began to cry, not knowing where to hide.

Snarky turned out to be a very sarcastic clown and started picking on people:

"I heard your mind started to wander and it didn't come back."

"I heard you took an IQ test and the results were negative."

"I heard your parents really hated you. Your bath toys were a toaster and a radio."

"You're so ugly, your mother had morning sickness after you were born."

Suddenly, Snarky turned to me.

"Hey, Charlie…" Everyone grew quiet and looked at me. "…I heard you dress to kill, and you cook the same way."

And then, everything went black.

When I awoke I saw three faces staring down at me: Bradley, Alex and…Funky? I screamed.

"Where am I?"

"You're home," said Alex.

But, I thought there was no place like home, and now my home had Funky in it. Funky and his toothless grin.

"What happened to me?

"You were at a party and fainted," said Alex.

"Funky, what are you doing here? We went out in 12th grade. I don't understand." He was wearing a tight fitting button-down black shirt and tight jeans. He was holding a bunch of carnations.

As I continued to look up at the three faces, it suddenly dawned on me what all three had in common. I didn't want a relationship with any of them. Bradley like it or not, was in bed with the Mafia, Alex was sharing his bed with someone else, but decided he'd rather share my bed, and Funky had made a virtual bed in a cartoon bubble with me and him lying in it. Eww!

"I need you all to leave. Thank you for being here, but, I need to be by myself."

"Savannah is downstairs," moped Bradley.

"I'm sorry, Bradley, but you can't stay here anymore. The Mafia's not just after you, now they're after me, too."

"The Mafia?" Funky tried to whistle through his front teeth, but it didn't work. "I just came to see if you wanted me to fix your rear windshield. I heard it got blown to pieces."

"We still need to talk about, you know," said Bradley.

"Alex, you're still working for the DA, so I need to talk to Bradley alone."

"DA?" Funky got excited. "Why did we ever break up, Charlie? You're like one of them Charlie's Angel's. Action packed...in every way. Do you remember how we used to do it in the Dodge Dart? Fucking bomb!"

I heard a knock on my bedroom door. "Can I come in?" asked Savannah.

"Yes! Come in! Thanks for making sure I'm okay, guys. I'd like to talk to Savannah alone now."

Alex looked really hurt. But, he couldn't have it both ways. He couldn't expect me to share the details of my investigation if he was working with someone who wanted to put me in jail. And, even though he told me he didn't love the woman he was living with, he was still living with her. It wasn't fair to lead me on.

The three left, looking very dejected.

"Hi honey, ah bought you a cup of chamomile tea."

"What happened? The last thing I remember, I was staring at a huge white pasty face....I can't even talk about it."

"You fainted. It's none of my business, but ah think you need to stay away from those tennis girls for awhile."

101

"Well, it wasn't their fault, it was the clown. The clown was so mean. This is my conundrum: I really don't like a lot of the tennis ladies, but I love tennis and I love competition. And, I really like playing with you."

"Honey, my mama always told me, 'a whistling woman and a crowing hen never comes to a very good end.' You take care, now."

As I tried to decipher that cryptic piece of advice, I fell into a fitful sleep.

CHAPTER 13

When I opened my eyes, I found a familiar set staring straight into mine.

"Bradley, you're still here."

"Your windshield, it wasn't Mafia. My guess it was someone trying to stop you from digging."

"How do you know it wasn't Mafia?" I noticed how all of Bradley's appendages were swinging freely now.

"I have my sources."

"You're a quick healer," I said.

"I'll make you some coffee, we have a lot to discuss."

When I walked into the kitchen, Bradley was standing on a step stool making me eggs. The aroma of freshly ground coffee brewing was comforting.

"Okay, you can stay. Sorry I was so grumpy."

"I know what it's like to feel that the whole world is against you." He handed me a plate of perfectly cooked eggs over easy, a piece of whole grain toast, and a mug of coffee. "I did some research on the two capsules you gave me. They're counterfeit."

"Counterfeit? How do you know?"

"Several things. I opened up one of the capsules and there was powder instead of small white pellets. There was also an expiration date stamped on the capsules with the month, day and year. Legit drugs have only the month and year. I sent one of the capsules to a lab. One of the active ingredients was sibutramine. The real drug, Alli, contains no sibutramine."

"What's sibutramine?"

"It's a stimulant and can lead to elevated blood pressure, stroke or heart attack."

"So, maybe the peanut chew wasn't poisoned, and the hamster simply died from eating one of these capsules. It was an accident, like the secretary said. Case closed."

"Maybe, maybe not. We won't know for sure until someone finds out about the autopsy." He gave me a look.

"It's on my to-do list, I'm sorry. I have other pressing issues on my mind, like not going to jail."

The doorbell rang several times. I looked through the peephole. Marshall! And, he was with that tramp. I opened the door.

Before I could say his name, Bradley, who was hiding beside the door, uttered, "Sonia!"

Who is Sonia, I thought? That was Gayle.

"Sonia?" Marshall looked at her.

The color drained from Gayle's face.

"Your boyfriend almost got me killed!" yelled Bradley.

"Boyfriend?" said Marshall. "Gayle is my wife."

"Well, she may be your wife, but she's also someone's girlfriend. Actually, she's a few guys' girlfriend. One of them was the guy that pummeled me at McSorely's pub in Ben Salem. The other guy is a big mahoof…that guy's boss. Sonia, I mean Gayle, knows what I'm talking about."

"He's lying," said Gayle. "I may look like someone he knows. But, I've never been to McSorely's Bar in my life."

"Did I say pub? My mistake. It's a bar. Thanks for correcting me."

"Marshall, why did you come here?" I asked.

"To pick up some of the boys' things. But, I think Gayle and I need to talk."

I closed the door.

"Bradley, you just blew your cover!"

"I know. But, I was shocked to see her."

"Are you sure it's her? I mean, this could help me get back custody of my kids."

"I'm pretty sure it's her. I mean, the last time I saw her she was wearing a g-string and pasties, and her hair was a lot longer and a different color."

"Bradley."

"I am almost 90%."

"Good enough for me. I need to let the judge know."

"And, I'm packing. I need to get out of here as soon as I can."

"Where will you go?"

"Just got a text from Edith," Bradley said looking at his cell phone.

We both looked at each other and shook our heads no. Things could never be bad enough to stay with Edith.

Against Savannah's better judgment I decided to mingle with the tennis girls once again and take Chad's "Butt-Busting" drill at Mill Creek. It was Sunday, and I decided that some good exercise was just what I needed. Between my car window being blown out and the clown drama I had just endured, I deserved some fun. Hopefully, some different girls would be at the drill.

As it turned out, a ton of girls had signed up for the "Butt" drill. So many girls that Eddie was teaching the drill, too. Ugh. I did not want to be on his court. While I was at the desk paying for the drill, I heard Eddie talking to Chad. "I'll bet you $20.00 that Connie and Collette don't last the whole time. Collette is always whining about some injury and Connie is so out of shape."

"Not now, Eddie" sighed Chad. Chad was looking at all the girls in amazement. "We need to figure out how we're going to divide everyone up. I'll take the 4.0s and you take the 3.5s."

Eddie gave him a disdainful look. "No, I want the 4.0s and you take the 3.5s. The 4.0's are more fun. Don't forget, I've been here longer than you."

Gary, who also taught, was wandering around the lobby and overheard. "The drill was Chad's idea and the girls signed up thinking they were going to be taught by Chad. Cindee shouldn't have signed up so many girls."

Chad took a buzzer used for timed matches off the desk. Everyone quieted down when they heard the buzzer.

"Ladies, everyone out to court 3 and we're going to divide you into three courts," Chad said.

I heard a lot of groans.

"We're going to switch courts every 30 minutes," Chad said.

Everyone walked out onto the courts. Luckily, I was one of the ones Chad picked to start out on his court. It was me, Andi, Barb, Jazzy, Maria Theresa and Devon. Barb wasn't talking to me and neither was Devon. And, these were my "teammates."

"We're not stopping for the next 30 minutes, so take your drinks now." Chad was not only a great teacher, but he was also funny, and did I mention lately that he was gorgeous? The combination made Eddie crazy because all the girls just wanted "privates" with Chad. I could see Eddie look at our court now and again.

We started out with reflex volleys, three against three. Then we were taught the correct footwork when tracing a lob and turning it from a defensive shot into an offensive one. The swinging volley approach was my favorite. It was a great way to get out your aggressions. I looked at the clock; it was way past 30 minutes.

"Offense-Defense" said Chad. "Charlie, you start with me." Our opponents had to win two out of three points to take my spot. But, nobody did. My strengths were that I was fast, had good court sense, was crafty and very consistent.

Finally, Eddie screamed over, "Aren't we switching yet?" Chad looked at me and shrugged. I could tell he was having fun with me as his partner.

"Okay. Ladies, everyone on my court go to Eddie's court."

For the next half hour I played on manic Eddie's court. Every ten minutes he would ask us: "Is everyone having a good time?" He was always marketing himself for the next drill. And, if he wasn't marketing, he was gossiping. I had been burned by Eddie a few years ago. I had sent him an email in confidence and he had forwarded it. Lesson learned, never put anything confidential in an email and never trust Eddie. He was a yenta.

Finally, the drill was over. Henry was behind the desk hanging up racquets he had just strung.

"Good afternoon, Charlotte. How's the investigation going? Have they found any other suspects?"

I was about to say that he should mind his own business. After all, he was a suspect in a crime and he actually served jail time. But, I promised Cindee I wouldn't say anything.

"Everyone is a potential suspect until they find out who did it," I said.

"But the cyanide, in your purse. Why were you carrying it?"

"Someone planted it in my purse," I said. I could feel my face burning.

"Innocent till proven guilty, Henry," said Chad, who had just walked up to the desk.

Why was Henry being so accusatorial? The only thing I could think of was that maybe it was him who did it and he was trying to cast aspersions on me. Maybe he was in cahoots with Nora and trying to bring down the club. I looked at Eddie who was schmoozing as many girls as he could. Maybe he did owe money to several girls on the Mood Swings team and couldn't pay them back. By poisoning the soup, he was betting that he could knock off those girls and if he ended up killing some other girls, oh well. I could see Eddie becoming that desperate. My mouth went dry. What was happening to me? My thoughts had become so draconian.

A whisper in my ear broke me out of my unsettling trance.

"Let's get something to eat," said Chad.

We walked out together and I could feel all eyes turn to us. It was raining fairly hard outside.

"Let's take my car," I said.

"I'll follow you. Where to?" Chad asked.

"There's a cute English pub on River Road," I said.

"I know the one."

He followed over my least favorite bridge, the Washington's Crossing Bridge. I drove like an old lady over the bridge, because it was so narrow, but I didn't care. It was always so nerve-wracking. The rain was coming down harder. An Escalade was moving towards me on the opposite lane. I silently cursed as I tried to anticipate how I was going to eke by the SUV. They might as well allow semi-trailers on this bridge. There was only a slim chance that my RAV4 could pass by the truck without becoming part Escalade. I channeled my Irish side and did a virtual cross. My Jewish side was too busy cogitating on the corned beef I knew I'd be ordering in the pub. My stomach was divided also: grumbling with hunger and filled with fear.

Suddenly, it became apparent to me that the truck was purposely not staying in its lane. It began to barrel right into me! I beeped my horn several times, but the truck wasn't stopping! It purposely sideswiped my car. I jerked my steering wheel to the right, trying to avoid it, and I crashed into the rail.

A split second later, I saw Chad running past my car with a gun. He started shooting at the driver in the truck. The truck zoomed past my car and sped off the bridge.

My SUV was sandwiched against the side railing. My whole body had been thrown toward the dashboard. Even though the airbags deployed, I still felt bruised and my head hurt. Chad opened the passenger's door. "Are you okay?" He gently helped me out of the car and into the passenger's seat of his car.

"Thanks for saving my life. Do you always carry a gun?"

"I'm licensed and you never know when you'll need to help a lady in distress."

We heard sirens and a police car driving toward us.

"That was quick," I said. When the cop got out of the car, I knew why I had gotten such good service. It was Alex.

"What happened? Charlie, can you show me your driver's license?" asked Alex.

"Driver's license?" Chad looked incredulous. "The poor girl almost got killed and you want to see her license?"

"If you give me any more lip, I'm going to give you a citation for disorderly conduct. This conversation is being recorded. Did you get the other vehicle's plates?" Alex asked.

"What are you kidding?" Chad asked. "I was trying to save Charlie. She was almost pushed off the bridge."

Alex started writing a ticket. "This is a citation for disorderly conduct. You have 14 days to respond."

Chad looked at the ticket. "$360?" He tore it up.

Alex pulled out his cuffs. Chad pulled out a wallet from his back pocket.

I could feel blood trickle down my face and my whole body felt bruised. 'Uh, hello?' I wanted to say. 'Remember me? I'm the traumatized one.' Maybe if I dangled one of my limp arms in front of them.

"Put away those cuffs, Mate," ordered Chad. Chad pulled out a card from his wallet and showed Alex. "Or, you'll be lucky to have a job in the morning."

Chad was speaking in an English accent now. Alex looked at the card and stared at me coldly. It was the same look he gave me when we first met at the club. He turned, got into his car and drove away.

All I could say to Chad was, "Mate?"

We sat in silence in Chad's car as we waited 20 minutes till my car was towed off the bridge. The tow person asked me if I had a garage I wanted it towed to. I was surprised; usually they just towed it to the nearest gas station. I don't know why, but I heard myself giving the address of Funky's gas station, "The Gas 'N' Go" in Langhorne. He'd been nice enough to fix my windshield, so I decided to give him the business. And, only that business, I shuddered, thinking of those missing teeth again.

"Do you want to go to the hospital?" Chad asked in his American accent.

"The jigs up, Chad. I know you're English. I don't want to go to the hospital."

"Well, luckily I was a pre-med major before…"

"Before you went to lie school?"

"Before I went to spy school. I'm an INTERPOL agent. Now do you…"

"INTERPOL agent? I thought you were a tennis pro? And, all of a sudden you have an English accent?"

"I can't say anything more now," Chad said, sternly.

"Wait a minute, you need to say a lot more now. INTERPOL is International police, right?"

"Right."

"So, you're here in sleepy Bucks County because…"

"Do you want me to drive you home?"

It was a stubborn standoff. I glared at him. I knew he was not going to be more forthcoming…at least on this precarious bridge in the pouring rain.

"No, Bradley might still be there. And, then he might let it slip to Edith that I was with you, whoever you are, and then, I would make the front cover of the Bucks Bugle three times in one month: "Mah Jongg Mom…murderer and Mata Hari." I mean, it's more news than Bucks County could ever hope to have in all its existence."

I made Chad laugh. He couldn't stop laughing.

"I don't think I've laughed in a year. It's so debilitating being 'round all those tennis girls, day in, day out…complaining, gossiping, flirting."

"Well, welcome to my world, except the last thing. Actually, Savannah sometimes flirts with me."

And then he kissed me. Wasn't that the title of an old song? I stopped thinking and let my mind enjoy Chad's caresses. He didn't care that I was bloody or sweaty or that most of my appendages were in a dangling state. He was incredibly passionate. I think we were both so relieved that we could let down our guard and finally trust someone.

We drove to Chad's apartment. He parked and took me in his arms, lifting me out of the car. Our lips were still locked as he keyed into his condo. He carried me upstairs to his bed and gently laid me down. He went into the bathroom and brought out a warm, wet washcloth and carefully cleaned my wounds. We looked at each other. He wanted to and I wanted to, too. But, my arms and legs started to really hurt. Damn!

"I'm going to make you a cup of tea. And then I'll bandage you up."

"It would be a lot sexier if you said tie," I smiled weakly.

"Maybe we'll do the S & M thing tomorrow…on our second date," he smiled back.

"So, if you're an agent, is Chad your real name?"

"No, it's Charlie."

"Charlie? Damn! What are we going to do?"

Charlie left me to ponder this dilemma. I wasn't able to ponder long because I heard loud shouting downstairs. I peaked through the door but couldn't see anything. I ran to the bathroom and looked out the window. Two cop cars. One of them was an undercover car, which looked like Alex's.

I quietly opened the bedroom and peaked down the stairs.

"You're not coming in here, mate. You have no jurisdiction over me," said Chad.

"We have a warrant for her arrest and I know she's here. She was with you about an hour ago," Alex said.

"I dropped her off at her house," Chad said.

"We checked the house and she's not there," Chad said.

"She could have not heard the bell."

"We spoke to the dwarf," the other cop said.

"Bloke's got a name, mate."

"We spoke to Bradley, and he said she hadn't come back from her drill," Alex said.

I mouthed the words fuck! I am fucked!

"Tahm to let you know who's boss, son. Mah name is Officer Kent, and we have a search warrant, issued by the DA, to search your house."

Chad grabbed the piece of paper and looked it over. "Do you have new evidence? She's just a suspect."

"A Grand Jury has indicted her. She can try and clear herself at her trial," said Alex. He was rubbing the handcuffs that were attached to his belt.

Handcuffs? "Fuck!

"Well," Chad said loudly, "If you have to check then check, but she's not here!"

The two cops pushed their way past Chad. Panic-stricken, I quickly looked for a place to hide. No way was I letting them take me before I could clear myself. Where could I go? I hobbled left, then right. I was slow as molasses and still in pain. I limped to the bathroom, opened the window, and somehow pulled myself out. Thankfully, I was able to close the window from the outside. The rain had not let up and the ledge was slick. I carefully sidestepped a few feet and felt myself slipping. I quickly latched onto a pipe that I saw. I clung for a few seconds but couldn't resist peaking inside. I sidestepped back to the window and squinted through the raindrops. I saw Alex and Oversize open up all the closets, rip the sheets off the bed and then look under it. Alex knelt down on the carpet. He put on rubber gloves, took a penknife off his belt and scraped something into an envelope. My blood? Was I dripping blood? They headed to the bathroom and I quickly sidestepped some more and pulled myself onto the roof. Funny how fear let's you do things you have no business being able to do. Good thing I was able to climb. As soon as I had pulled myself up, I heard the window open, then shut.

After what seemed like an eternity, I heard the front door slam. Still crouching on the roof, I saw Alex and Oversize talking, as they walked slowly back to their cars. I was hoping they wouldn't look up to the roof and thankfully they didn't. As soon as I saw them drive away, I inched my way back down to the ledge and sidestepped back to the window. Of course, it was stuck. I banged loudly and finally Chad opened the window. His face was white as he pulled me inside.

"It's official now, you were indicted for murder."

"I'm sorry if I got you in trouble."

"I'm not worried about me. They can't touch me. But, you…"

"They must have new evidence to indict. But, I thought it was all circumstantial."

"Look at you, you're drenched. Now I have to take your clothes off. You leave me no choice."

Chad gently peeled my clothes off and he took his off also. He turned the shower on and guided me in. We held each other in silence under the warm water. I knew he would be a great kisser, and he didn't disappoint me in all the places that received his kiss. He traced my nipples with his fingers. Man, good hands on the court and good hands on the... and suddenly I couldn't hold back any longer. I had the mother of all climaxes and felt every ounce of tension leave my body. I made sure Chad knew that I also had good hands and that my mouth was well equipped for other things than defiance and quick one-liners. He quickly came also.

"Care for a cup of tea?" Chad sighed happily.

The INTERPOL agent was back on the job again.

After we both dressed, I followed Chad-Charlie to the kitchen. He made me a cup of tea and gave me an English biscuit.

"Why didn't you turn me in?" I asked.

"I can't tell you what a relief it is to talk to someone in my normal accent."

"Chad...I mean Charlie...why didn't you turn me in?"

"Isn't it obvious?"

"I guess you like me, huh?"

"Well, after what we just did...I obviously like you! But, I also need you.....in an illegal way. No, that didn't come out quite right."

"That sounds kinky. I'll take it! You still haven't told me why you were pretending to be a pro at Mill Creek."

"As I told you, I work for INTERPOL. And, one of many things that INTERPOL investigates is tracking counterfeit drugs. It's a pandemic problem that causes millions of deaths in many third world countries. Unfortunately, counterfeiting is extremely profitable and not too hard to pull off."

"I still don't understand why you're pretending to be a pro."

"Before I became an agent, I was actually a professional tennis pro, so it was a natural cover for me."

"And you're here because...."

"I'm following the money. We have bank records from this zip code. Money is being funneled in to a bank account somewhere in this area."

"Where specifically are these drugs being sold?"

"Sweden to Singapore. For example, counterfeit drugs make up about 6% of total seizures. That's how dangerous these drugs are. And it doesn't stop there. People are given fake drugs for life threatening diseases like HIV, malaria, TB, and on and on."

"Oh no. That's awful."

"Sales average over $75 billion. If you're looking to make big, easy money, counterfeiting is the perfect industry. But, it's hard to catch someone in the act of producing the drugs. Warehouses open and close very quickly."

"But, why specifically Mill Creek?"

"Mill Creek is in the area code. And, like I said, I used to play professional tennis, so it was the perfect cover for me. The fact that there are so many weird people and murders that keep surrounding the club is just a bonus."

"Wait a minute. Bradley said that Bucky may have been killed with a counterfeit drug. He may have eaten a peanut chew laced with sibutramine. The drug was called Alli," I said.

"Who's Bucky?"

"A hamster."

"Who's Bradley?"

"A dwarf…I mean he's an investigative reporter who is a dwarf. He's hiding out at my place because the Mafia is after him."

Chad looked really confused.

"Bradley sat on a stripper."

"Oh, that clears everything up," Chad laughed. "Oy, my first lead and it's a hamster? Who would want to kill a hamster? And why with a counterfeit drug?"

"It was an accident. That's what the secretary of the school told me. One of the kids fed Bucky a diet pill by accident. They thought they were giving him vitamins."

"Well, then I need to interview the kid that bought that bottle in."

"She doesn't know which kid. Just that a kid did it."

"Do you have one of the capsules?" Chad asked.

"I gave them to Bradley."

"We need to go back to the school and talk with the secretary and the teacher. Just want to confirm what happened. I need to find out which kid bought the bottle of pills to school."

I suddenly got a text from Edith.

"Spoke 2 B. Heard u were indicted. Cops looking 4 u."

I text back: "plz don't fire me. Need job. Trying 2 clear myself."

"do u have access 2 computer? need 2 video chat."

"She wants to video chat, " I said to Chad. "Do you have a computer with iChat?"

Chad gave me his computer and we set up the iChat. Egads! Edith was even scarier looking via video.

"Charlie! I'm going to start a new column. I'm calling it: 'Notes from the Underground.'" She always gestured wildly when she was excited. She took a long puff from her plastic cigarette holder and held it in for what seemed like hours. I was waiting for her head to explode. I imagined the machinations of Edith's mind to be like the inner workings of gears inside a cartoon clock: smoothly and methodically cranking out ideas. Finally, she let out a huge cloud of cigarette smoke. "I want it gritty, I want it real. It's going to be fantastic. Unlike anything any paper has done before…urban observations from a…a…tennis playing, Bucks County mom on the lam."

"But, won't you get into trouble when the cops know that you've spoken to me and didn't tell them."

"You let me handle the cops. I've dealt with tougher customers. I'll have Stanley wire you money. You just keep emailing me your stories, and stay in the shadows, Charlie. I'll be in touch."

"She's fantastic," laughed Chad.

I gave him a look. "How am I going to stay in the shadows? Wait a minute, my costumes I use when I'm critiquing a restaurant. I need to go to my house and get my costumes."

"We'll get your friend Bradley to pack up your disguises and we'll meet him somewhere."

"Let me just check my email." I had over 300 messages in my Inbox. One of the subjects was "Districts." I clicked on it.

GIGI ARNOLD

"Let's get pumped for Districts, girls! We are playing the #1 team, the Mood Swings, July 15th. Here's the line-up:
    1st Court: Barb/Kathy
    2nd Court: Charlie/Savannah
    3rd Court: Elaine/Jen
    1st Singles: Devon
    2nd Singles: Mary Ellen
We (and staff at Mill Creek) have all been invited to a Districts After Party at Jazzy's house. A party at the enemy camp…should be interesting."

I logged off. "How am I going to play in Districts if the cops are trying to find me?"

"You'll wear a disguise."

"I really want to play. Grace sat me during Districts last year and I was totally humiliated."

"You take this stuff pretty seriously, huh?"

"Could be very dramatic, though. I win my match and then the cops handcuff me…on the court…and drag me off to jail. Great for my underground column, bad for my love-life."

"We'll have to give you some special training to get you ready for the competition." Chad kissed me.

After the special training session, Chad left to teach a drill at Mill Creek and I decided to check out Kabbalah and Kibbutz. One of the perks of INTERPOL was that Chad was given several cars. He let me drive one of his. First stop was a costume shop. I left wearing a long, blonde wig and big dark sunglasses. I was also wearing a mini skirt, 2 layered undershirts and pumps. My goal was to look 20 years younger to throw off the cops. But, as I looked at my reflection in the store window, I somehow managed to look 20 times more ridiculous. No matter. I didn't look anything like me and that's all I cared about.

116

CHAPTER 14

Kabbalah and Kibbutz, which was located on a side street in New Hope, turned out to be both congested and eclectic. Wall to wall bottles of liquid "potions" lined one wall. I'm sure there was a politically correct name for the jars, but the oils being poured and mixed in small vials by the witches seemed very potion-like. The other part of the store had crammed bookshelves, mystic chatchkahs, and a few tiny tables. I guess that's where the 'Kibbutz' part came in. But, it was hard to see how any good gossip could be generated in a store that was so cluttered.

Phil and several other witches were busy pulling various bottles and dried herbs off the shelves. Were they Wiccans or witches and what was the difference? Some were pouring oils on candles and others were conversing with their customers.

A sales person suddenly approached me. "Can I help you?" She looked very goth, with purple and black streaked hair, black lipstick, black nails, nose rings, lip rings, not gonna guess where else rings, and a long, black dress, finished with funky black military boots.

"Uh, no, I'm going to wait for Phil," I said. She scared me.

"Can I get you a cup of tea while you wait?" she asked. All that was missing was "my pretty" at the end of her question; that, and green face paint.

Meanwhile, Phil was still talking with a woman. She was thin but curvaceous, and wore a tight t-shirt, short shorts and high heels. Her hair was its own "Little Shop of Horrors." Hey lady, the 70's called, and they want their big hair back.

I decided to meander around the store. I picked up several books. The first was called, "Kabbalah with Challah: Breaking Bread with the Dead." I read a page or two then impatiently looked over at Phil. The lady he was talking to finally turned around. My heart skipped a beat. Under those sunglasses, it looked like Brenda Cappuccino. She was Eddie's wife!

"Hi, Brenda," I said. Whoops! Forgot that I was in disguise.

"Oh, hi," Brenda barely looked at me. She was holding three candles and a few vials of oils and quickly made her way out of the store.

I nonchalantly made my way towards the counter. "Phil?" Phil didn't know who I was.

"Can I help you with something?" He was wearing a long, dark coat.

"It's me, Charlie," I whispered.

"Charlie? What are you doing here?"

"What are you doing here? I thought you only worked nights?"

"Exterminating has been kind of slow lately, people cutting back. I asked for some extra hours."

"The woman you just sold those candles to. Was that Brenda Cappuccino?"

"Hey, aren't the cops looking for you?" Phil was looking at the receipt of the last customer. "Robin told me they have enough circumstantial evidence now to indict."

"Shhh. I'm staying in the shadows, just till I can clear myself."

"The credit card says 'Edward Cappuccino.' Boy, was she an odd duck."

As opposed to you and all the other sales staff here, I wanted to point out.

"Why was she odd?"

"Well, for starters, she was such a nervous Nelly."

"What type of candles did she buy?"

"Why do you want to know? That's sort of private."

"Please, Phil."

"Well, you can't tell anyone this. People come in here and tell us their problems, and we pride ourselves on keeping everything they say confidential. But, being that you're trying to clear yourself of murder but trying to stay one step ahead of the law, so you don't have to go to jail again and …"

"Yes, yes…" I didn't need a recap of all my woes.

"She bought three candles, one orange, one green and one yellow."

"That's an odd combination."

"You have got to keep this confidential, Charlie. I don't want anyone coming after me for telling you this."

"I promise you, Phil. I won't say a word."

"She bought those candles to bring her husband gambling luck. She said that they were hundreds of thousands of dollars in debt and he begged her to let him bet one more time…to pay off their debt to the Mafia. So, she wanted to buy candles to bring him luck this last time."

"She told you that?"

My heart skipped a beat again. Gambling luck? Cindee was right. Eddie had a gambling problem and that would explain why his wife acted so peculiar. She was probably so sick with worry about the debt that her last resort was to buy these candles, hoping they would bring Eddie luck.

"How do the candles give you luck?" I asked.

"You draw a dollar sign on the green candle, an arrow pointing to the right on the orange candle, and an arrow pointing to the left on the yellow candle. Then you anoint them with a magnetic oil."

"Magnetic oil?"

"You soak a magnet in vegetable oil for 3 days. You say a different incantation when you light each candle. Like, when you light the green candle you would say, 'Money come and money grow. Money green, to me now flow.' And, there's more. Do you need to know that?"

"No, I think I know enough to know Eddie's desperate."

"She also bought three tiger-eye stones that you're supposed to keep with your pocket change to increase gambling luck."

"Anything else?" I asked.

"Do chants count?" Phil asked.

"Chants?"

"She asked me if there was a candle of lost items. I told her no but there was a chant: 'Keeper of what disappears, Hear me now - open our ears. Find for me what I now seek, By Moon, Sun, Wind, Fire, Earth, and Sea.'" She left her thong at some guys house last night and she was in a panic. This guy is another tennis pro who knows Eddie. He claims he can't find the thong. She's gonna go to his house and use the chant. You wouldn't believe the stuff people tell me."

"So, she's cheating on Eddie with another pro? Did she tell you the pro's name?" Please don't tell me the pro is Chad, I thought. Man, that guy can't keep his doodle in his pants for a second.

"No, she didn't mention his name."

"Phil, do you remember the vial of oil that was taken from my desk and dumped in Lilly's soup?"

"I spent a night in jail for it. Yeah, I remember."

"Well, I still don't know who took it from my desk, but I wanted to find out who bought oils from your store that day....or that week."

"Those oils could have been bought any time before that happened."

"You're right. But, if you could just look up that week... the week of June 14th."

Phil went on the computer and printed out purchases.

"Hey Phil, what are you doing?" the manager asked, twirling his black cape. The cape, coupled with his thin, pencil mustache, made him look like Zorro.

"My manager," Phil whispered to me.

"All purchases are confidential," said the manager.

"There was a murder that took place at Sacre Bleu! and oils from your store were found in the soup that killed Lilly Werthenheim," I said to the manager.

"How do you know they were oils purchased from this store? All purchases made here are confidential. Phil, I'll take that sheet. You want to keep your job, right?"

Phil nodded.

"Then don't let me see you giving out private information again."

"It's my fault," I said to the manager.

The manager's attention turned to another sales person helping a customer. Phil printed me out another sheet when the manager went into the storage room.

"Thanks, Phil." I gave him kiss.

I discreetly looked at the names. Surprisingly, a few people from my office were on the list: Robin, I knew. But, Inge and Stanley, and Julie Quinn? As puzzling as that was, at least I could confirm that Eddie had a definite motive for poisoning the soup. He definitely had a large gambling debt and was 'betting' that Andi would eat the soup when her team ate first. He obviously didn't care who else went down with her. If she were dead, he would never have to pay her back. Grace was just an unlucky casualty in his eyes. But, where would he have gotten the cyanide?

"One other thing," I asked Phil, who looked unhappy that our conversation hadn't finished. "I noticed you were pouring herbs into vials. Are poisoned mushrooms in any of those herbs?"

"Yes, we sometimes use them. But we obviously don't advocate drinking the herbs, Charlie. They're strictly for enhancing the strength of a candle."

When I got in my car, I called Chad. I gave him a recap and then asked, "But how did Eddie get the cyanide? It's not like you can buy it at Walmart. Or can you? It seems like you can buy everything else at Walmart."

"It does seem that an extraordinary amount of poison is being generated from and around the club," Chad said.

I suddenly remembered my car was ready. "Listen, I got a call from Funky. My car's ready, but I don't want to pick it up alone."

"Why is that?"

"You know why. The police are looking for me. Which isn't exactly the main reason. I don't want to be alone with him. Funky said he found some pictures in the glove compartment of a car he was inspecting, that he said would make me 'hot.' He really wants to show them to me."

Chad laughed.

"It's not funny. He's perverted and gross."

"You're undercover, I don't think you can go anyway. The cops will be looking for your car. You'll drive my car and drop me off. I have a feeling Funky won't want to show me the hot pictures."

I met Chad at his condo…for another special training session…and then we headed to the Gas 'N' Go in Langhorne. I stayed in the car while Chad went into Funky's office to get my keys and pay for the repairs. Chad walked out of the office and texted me. "u need 2 sign."

"Then leave car" I texted back.

Funky tapped on the car window and I squeaked. Where did he come from?

"Hi Charlie. I know it's you under there."

"Hi. I heard I need to sign for the car."

"Hey, aren't the cops looking for you?"

"Funky, listen. You can't tell the cops. Thanks for repainting my car, by the way."

"Is that guy with you?"

"Yeah, he's…uh…my boyfriend."

Poor guy. Funky looked really dejected. I signed for the car and quickly left. I saw Funky running after the car.

"Wait! Wait! I forgot the pictures," he screamed.

But, I didn't want to stop. I followed Chad to an empty lot and replaced my plates with fake ones.

"Let's cut up the plate," he said.

I opened my glove compartment to put the pieces in and saw four pictures. So this is what he was screaming about. I stuck my head out the window. "Chad! Come here!"

Chad opened the passenger's side and sat down. He looked at the naked couple in various pornographic poses.

"Friends?" Chad asked.

"Funky must have left them in my glove compartment by mistake.," I said. "Surely, these are the kinds of pictures he likes to keep on his desk."

We both stared at the pictures for an awkwardly long, length of time.

"Anyone you know?" we both asked each other finally.

"You know, I think I do know them. It took me a bit, because I had met them with their clothes on," I said.

"Meaning, you sometimes meet people without their clothes on?" Chad smiled.

"Hey, don't get me started on naked encounters. How many tennis girls have you slept with?"

"You were saying you know these people?" Chad quickly got on topic again.

"The guy is the principal at Langhorne Elementary and the woman is his secretary. She lied to me. She told me at the funeral that it was Andrea Birnbaum that was having the affair with Principal Paul. But, I can see it's really her." I said.

"Why would she lie about that?" Chad asked.

"I don't know. But, she's also the one that found the..." I made quote marks. "...'vitamins' that she said were fed to Bucky."

"Something is up with this secretary. We need to talk to her now," Chad said.

"What's her name? Julie Quinn, that's it. The school's only about a mile from here," I said.

"I'll drive. We'll leave your car here," Chad said.

We drove to the school and went directly to the Principal's office. There was another woman sitting at the desk where I had first met Julie.

"We'd like to talk with Julie Quinn, please," I said.

"Julie doesn't work here anymore. She…"

Just then Principal Paul came barreling out of his office. It's like he had a sixth sense when anyone wanted to ask a personal question about the school.

"I told you no more questions the first time you came here. I'm going to call the police."

How did he recognize me under my disguise? Yeesh.

"I am the police, mate." Chad flashed both his INTERPOL badge and his dazzling English smile. "We're following up a conversation we had with Ms. Quinn. She gave my friend, here, two 'vitamin' capsules she said she found in a classroom. She said the capsules were fed to Bucky by mistake. Turns out they're counterfeit drugs. We'd like to find out how she got them."

The principal went white. "So Bucky was poisoned?"

"We need to talk to Ms. Quinn," said Chad firmly.

"Both Ms. Quinn and I decided that it would be best if she didn't work here anymore."

"Could this be why?" I showed him the x-rated pictures.

"Where did you get these?"

The principal tried to grab them from my hands but I pulled them away just in time. All those reflex volley drills and $85 dollar lessons finally paid off. I smiled with satisfaction.

"You had no idea these were being taken?" I asked.

"No. Okay, yes. They were taken on a tripod. But, this is the first time I've seen them." He hesitated a minute. "So, I cheated on my wife once. But, it was just once. What's that got to do with anything?"

"Anyone else that you've been with…'just once?'" asked Chad.

Paul motioned for us to follow him into his office. He slammed the door shut.

"I don't know why my infidelities are any of your business. What does any of this have to do with Bucky? Cheating on my wife is not a crime."

"Your cheating could have led to a crime. These pictures could very well be blackmail pictures," I said.

"I did sleep with somebody else that Julie knew. And, that's all I'm going to say without a lawyer."

"We'd like to speak with the custodian," said Chad.

"I'd like to speak with him, too. He didn't come into work today…again," Paul said angrily.

"Julie said she found the capsules when she was helping the custodian move a file cabinet out of the classroom," I said.

The principal burst out laughing.

"What's so funny?" Chad asked.

"Julie wouldn't do anything that would ruin her nails. Well, almost anything…" Paul smiled.

What a perverted bastard, I thought.

"Let's go," Chad said to me.

As we headed out the door, we saw Paul pick up the phone.

"I'm calling the police. I know they're looking for you," he sneered at me.

We ran to Chad's car and quickly pulled out of the parking lot.

"Where to?" I asked.

"We need to find Julie," said Chad.

I called information but her number was unlisted.

Chad hit the number 1 on the speed dial of his navigation system. "Sabine? I need the phone number and address of a Julie Quinn in Langhorne, Pennsylvania."

"So that's Sabine? You needed to call France for this?"

"Shh!" he whispered back. "Phone number is 215-555-3826. Address is 4224 Kelly Court, Southampton."

And then he said something that sounded a little too sweet and involving in French, like: "I will be with you as soon as I solve this little counterfeit thing and then I will be able to ditch this neurotic American girl." Yes, that's probably what he said. How could I possibly compete with someone named Sabine? Chad punched Julie's number in the Nav system, and we arrived at Julie's house in about 15 minutes.

"Let me talk to her," Chad said. "I'm afraid if she recognizes you, she won't open the door." Chad straightened my wig and gave me a quick kiss before he got out of the car.

He rang the bell and knocked on the door. Waited a few minutes and then made his way to the back of the house. After about 20 minutes, I was about to burst with curiosity. Finally, I saw him make his way towards the car.

"What did she say?"

"She wasn't there. I picked the back door lock and broke in. Then the alarm went off so I had to deprogram that." He showed me a magnetic gizmo.

"Bond...James Bond," I said in a very serious British accent. "All we need is some pictures of us falling into the greasy hands of Funky," I shuddered.

We drove back to the "Gas & Go" where we had left my car, but Alex and his partner were there. They were walking around, circling the car, so we drove past and headed to my house. I would have to pick up my car some other time.

There was one thing worse than having a cop on your tail, and it was having a jealous cop on your tail. Since I made it clear to Alex that it wouldn't be right to still see him because he was still in a relationship, he had become all business. He was now the humorless cop that I first met at the club.

I texted Bradley that we were on our way so he could have the box with my disguises ready as well as a box of my tennis clothes. I didn't need a lot of dressy clothes. I was wearing capris, tank tops and sandals almost everyday. As we pulled into my driveway, he threw the boxes and my racquets in the back seat. I looked at the racquets and looked at Bradley.

"Just in case you get in a fight with one of your tennis ladies!" Bradley smiled.

I missed my house. And, I really missed my kids. I was homesick for them. Thank goodness Marshall was going to Visiting Day. If I went, I would surely be arrested.

"Thanks, Bradley. I owe you."

"No problem. I have good news."

"At least someone has good news," I said.

"You remember the dancer whose lap I fell on?"

"Of course."

"Well, she told the Mafia Boss, Frank Genoa, aka her boyfriend, that me, sitting on her lap was just a mistake."

"Why now? Why didn't she tell him that in the first place?"

"Even though it was just an accident, she wanted to seem desirable, that's why she didn't tell him. She wanted to make him jealous."

"So, what prompted her to do it now?"

"You ready for this one? It was your ex, Marshall, that made her do it. The dancer who fell on my lap was the lady I saw at the door at your house. Gayle Ricci."

"No."

"Yes."

"So, the Mafia's not after me anymore," said Bradley, looking visibly relieved.

"I guess this means you can safely move out."

"Yeah. I'll be out in about an hour. I didn't have much when I moved in."

I smiled. "I know. You're like a new man, Bradley. No broken bones and no contract out on your life."

"See you at the next staff meeting," he said. "If you're not in jail first," he muttered under his breath. But, I heard him.

I grimaced at the thought of another staff meeting. I guess being on the lam did have its advantages.

I opened the car door and bent down to give Bradley a kiss. Chad and I waved good-bye, then we drove to his condo in silence. Finally, Chad spoke.

"I feel obliged to tell you there is a Demo Day tomorrow at the club."

"A Demo Day. Oh, man. I love Demo Days. I hate being on the lam." This was when being on the lam was not an advantage. Demo Day is when a representative from a major racquet company brings their new line of racquets to a club. And, there're drills, a great lunch, and games where you can win prizes like everything from a new racquet to t-shirts and cans of balls. All FREE!

"What company is coming?"

"Companies. Prince, Wilson, Yonex, Head, Babolat…"

"Oh, man! Companies? I have to go. I'll wear a disguise. I can also be a fly on the wall. Find out if people are talking about me."

"Have you decided what you're going to do about Districts?"

"I'm going to play….in disguise."

"You can't disguise your name." Chad gave me a very skeptical look.

"I'm playing. I didn't get a chance to play last summer. And, I'm going to play this summer. Uh, oh." In the rearview mirror I saw Alex's unmarked cop car and he was with his partner. "He is unrelenting…like a bad rash."

"We'll lose him. No worries," smiled Chad.

Chad did some fancy car maneuvers and we quickly lost Alex.

"Bond, James Bond," I said again.

We both laughed. But, I was worried. Sooner or later, it seemed inevitable that I'd be caught.

CHAPTER 15

I had never seen the parking lot at the club so full. I had to park on a side street. Demo Day was always a big event. I had decided to wear a blunt cut, blond wig, with tortoiseshell glasses. As I climbed up the steps to the club, I saw Collette smoking. Could not believe she was wearing a scarf. It was 90 degrees out. She was on her cell phone, talking in French and fiddling with her scarf. She seemed upset. What was she saying? Hmm, if only I spoke French, than I could be a "French Fly on the wall." I smiled at my little joke.

I proceeded into the club and walked up to the desk to sign in. Cindee, as usual, was manning the desk by herself and seemed frantic. She was handling the phones, while signing people in. I waited till she hung up.

"Hi, I'd like to sign in."

"Name?" Cindee asked.

I was stunned and stumped. I had forgot to think of a name.

"Your name?"

"Oh, sorry. I'm just getting over an ear infection." Why wasn't a name coming to me? I stared at all the displays of tennis clothes. "Nike…"

"Nike?" Cindee gave me a peculiar look.

"Nikki Topper," I said in my best Australian accent. Didn't Nike sound like Nikki in Australian?

"Oh, you're from Australia," Cindee smiled.

"Crikey! Yes, I am." I smiled back. Man, I am such an idiot. It's not enough that I have to fake what I look like. Now I have to fake my accent, too.

"New to this area? We have a lot of great tennis programs here."

Thankfully the phone rang. "Mill Creek tennis. Cindee speaking."

Before I began my mingling, I needed to use the ladies room. The ladies locker room was downstairs. Unfortunately, I had to pass Henry's office where he strung racquets to get to the bathroom. As I briskly walked past his office, I could see he was in an animated conversation with Gary. I stopped just past the office to see if I could hear anything. The door was barely ajar.

"....a friggin' $15 bucks an hour, that's all I'm askin'," screamed Henry. "Have you forgotten that I was the stringer for the Davis Cup team for 10 years? And..."

"And, that you were arrested for smuggling drugs? And, that Nora personally saw how you "delivered" the drugs to the players. And, how a player died because of you. You had given him counterfeit amphetamines."

"A man's gotta make a profit," said Henry. There was no remorse in his voice. "And, you can't prove they were counterfeit. Or, that he died because they were counterfeit."

"As a favor to you, Nora and I never went to the cops. You should be paying us! How do I know that you had nothing to do with the poisoning at the club? You had connections then. What would make me think you don't have them now? It was only 5 years ago that you were in jail. I'm thinking that Nora asked you to poison the soup to further damage the club's reputation. Between the leaky roof and the travel teams not wanting to play here now...we are in a shit-load of financial trouble. So, a raise is out of the question," Gary said.

"You'll be sorry, Gary."

Henry resumed stringing the racquet he was working on. Gary stormed out of the room.

I quickly slipped into the ladies locker room. I got a text from Chad. "Your x is here w/partner."

"Marshall is here with Gayle?" I text back, puzzled. I thought he left her. And, what was Marshall doing here?

"No. Alex the cop and sidekick."

Good time to begin writing, "Notes from the Underground." I quickly knocked off 500 words on my Net Book and sent them to Edith. I ended with, "Wondering if anybody else will inconveniently show up when I'm trying to stay incognito and fake an accent?"

I went to the bathroom, and when I got out I saw Andi on her cell. She looked upset. Why was everyone so upset today? She saw me and hung up.

" Hi. Is everything ok?" Why couldn't I keep my mouth shut when I was undercover?

"I can't believe I'm telling a stranger this," she said.

I could, because women in ladies rooms will tell strangers anything. It's a weird phenomenon about women. I can't tell you how many times I'll be washing my hands in the ladies room and a discussion will start about menopause and constant peeing, or period troubles, or who had a c-section, I was even asked to tease a celebrity's wife's hair once in the ladies room at a posh party in New York City.

"But, I am so angry," Andi continued. "I lent one of the pros here some money because he said he was in real trouble and needed to pay someone back right away. Well, he finally paid me back, two months later, but he wrote me a bad check. I was just on the phone with the bank. I had deposited that check in my team's charity fund. That money was supposed to go to underprivileged kids. We had ordered some new tennis nets and a few air conditioning units for the pro shop that this check was supposed to cover. He should be ashamed of himself."

"Which pro?" I asked, hopefully.

"I really shouldn't say. I'll just tell you that this guy never met a bet he didn't like."

I got the chills. I knew she was referring to Eddie. That would confirm what Cindee said about him and also why Eddie's wife had bought the candles and oils. What a scumbag.

"Whoever it is, he sounds like a real shonky," I said, hoping I'd used the word right.

"Hey, where're you from?"

"Melbourne. Just moved here."

"Too bad. A lot of shonky's here," smiled Andi. "Well, off to the bank. I need to take care of moving some money now. I can't even stay for the Demo Day. Nice meeting you."

Andi left, forgetting to take her tennis bag. I picked it up and was about to run after her when I noticed a picture jutting out from one of the zippered pockets. I took a look and almost fell over. It was Andi naked with Principal Paul! Unfortunately, there was no time to sit and absorb this. I needed to get upstairs and sign in for the drills. I quickly scooted past Henry's office and proceeded up the stairs.

I became increasingly nervous that someone would recognize me. I walked past the reception desk, waving to Cindee, who was on the phone. I couldn't help but notice a giant-sized poster of the Mood Swings that sat on an easel. They stood in front of a banner that read: "Serving Children in Africa's Malawi. All contributions help fund a tennis school for underprivileged children." Three large bins sat in front of the signs for gently used tennis racquets, clothes and balls. Something struck me odd about the sign, but I couldn't put my finger on it. A few other girls were also staring at the picture.

"Poor Plug. Poor Grace. They would have loved to have been in this picture."

"I know, it must be killing them," I blurted out. The inappropriate joke just fell out of my mouth. In my defense, I did mention earlier on that I have a history of blurting out inappropriate things.

The two girls looked at me in horror, shook their heads and walked away.

I saw a table filled with mini glasses of wine. I took three and quickly chugged them down. Much better. Keep mouth shut, I kept repeating to myself. I took a look out onto the courts. I could see the reps of the different racquet lines setting up their racquets. The drills were to start in 10 minutes. I knew almost everyone here. I decided to walk where my team was huddled.

"....but if she doesn't play who is Savannah going to play with?" asked Barb.

"Yeah, they're undefeated. She has to play. That would be a definite win," said Devon.

"Savannah, have you spoken with Charlie? How can I think about my line-ups if she doesn't return my emails?" Elaine said.

"I think y'all are as happy as a dead pig in the sunshine," Savannah admonished.

"What the hell does that mean?" asked Devon.

"That's what we like to say in the South when someone doesn't grasp or worry what's goin' on....the severity of the situation. Charlie is wanted for two murders and the only thing y'all can think about is wanting her to play in a tennis tournament?"

"This is Districts, Savannah," said Barb. "It's different."

"Yeah, if she's not in jail yet, she should play. And, she didn't even show up for practice yesterday," Jen said. "I think that's selfish."

"Well, I'll be dern," said Savannah, shocked at Jen's response.

I was equally stunned. Jen had turned into a monster. And, she used to be my best friend. I guess the need to win could turn anyone.

"We're a team. And, if Charlie wants to stay on this team she's got to play," insisted Elaine.

"If she's not in jail," said Mary Ellen. "I mean, that would be her only excuse."

"Of course. I mean, if she's in jail, she obviously can't play," Elaine said.

Everyone laughed. I was mortified. Then they turned to me.

"Who are you?" asked Devon suspiciously.

"I wouldn't put it past the Mood Swings to hire someone to spy on us," said Collette, as she adjusted her scarf.

"Nikki Topper. Just moved here from Australia," I said smiling, trying to channel the accent. I kept thinking about all the Australian pros I had heard in interviews on television.

The girls got very excited.

"From Australia? Anyone who lives there is practically born a pro," said Jen.

"What's your rating?" asked Elaine.

"Crikey! The last time I was rated I think I was a 5.0."

The group, who were 4.0's looked deflated. I would not be able to join their USTA team.

"But, maybe she could be a sub for our travel team?" Barb suggested.

The group got excited again.

"Can we get your email and cell number? We have a travel team that plays out of this club and it doesn't matter what you're rated," said Elaine.

She got out her cell phone to get my information, so I had to think quick.

"Oh, there's someone I need to have a chin wag with. I'll talk to you later," I said. Chin Wag? Darn I was a good. Where did I pull that out of?

The group watched me wander off as I pretended to look for someone. Just as I decided to try and infiltrate the Mood Swings huddle, Eddie yelled that the drills were starting.

"On my court....Collette, Jazzy, Maria Theresa, Ginger, Tammy, Andi, and Jessie." The girls followed Eddie to court 1.

Chad was flipping through his clipboard. My heart started to beat faster. Even though Chad and I made love, I still had a crush on him.

"Elaine, Jazzy, Collette, Savannah, Devon, Mary Ellen, Barb, and...Nike?"

"That's Nikki, " I gave Chad a look. "I'm from Australia." I gave Chad another look.

"Oh, Nikki. My fault. Sorry. Girls, we're on court 2," Chad said.

Luke, another pro, proceeded to call the girls on his court. "On court 3....Ellen, Sue, Steffi...."

As I was about to walk onto the court, I did a double take when I heard the name Steffi. Was that Steffi Scapelli? She had recognized me in my Rastafarian disguise at Mount Fuji, hopefully, she wouldn't recognize me now. I walked right past her and luckily she didn't say anything.

Each pro had been assigned a different racquet company. Chad's court was Head. A rep from Head helped us pick the right racquet for our game.

"I heard you were from Australia?" the rep said to me.

"Crikey! Yeah," Could I say anything but crikey? What else did Australian people say?

"Did you see Johnny Feller?" The rep asked me.

"Who?"

"Johnny Feller. He's from Australia. Ranked 450th on the tour. He's here representing Yonex. He's coming after the drills and doing half hour private lessons. I'm sure he'll get a kick out of meeting a fellow countryman.

More like he'll just kick me when he finds out I'm a fake.

Thankfully, for the next couple of hours, I was able to forget all my worries in the various drills and games. I couldn't wait to tell Chad my bombshell information: that the other woman Paul had an affair with was Andi.

Finally, it was time to eat. I was drenched in sweat and starving. Unfortunately, nothing really affected my appetite. Not even prospective jail time. The buffet table was covered with an enormous hoagie, a huge fruit salad, and a cake shaped like a tennis racquet. I gathered a big plate of food and was about to bite into my sandwich, when I saw Roscoe saunter into the club. A cameraman, lugging lights and various cases, followed him.

Nothing affected my appetite, that is, but Roscoe. I put down my hoagie. And, where was Alex and Oversize? There were too many danger zones. I needed to get out of here.

"There she is now!" I heard the Yonex rep say.

I felt a tap on my shoulder and turned around. I was staring at several baby blues: Johnny Feller, who was standing next to the rep, Alex, Oversize and Chad.

Uh, anyone else want to see my cover blown and then dragged off in handcuffs? I was starting to feel like this was déjà vu again, when the vials of cyanide were found in my purse, and I was interrogated by the same cops.

"Cheers, Nikki," smiled Johnny. He handed me a pair of new tennis shoes, made by Yonex. "Aussie, Aussie, Aussie…."

"Oy, oy, oy," I chanted back, trying to smile. I knew this chant only because several of my kids' counselors were from Australia and they always yelled this during lunch, a competitive sport, or in the bunk…actually anywhere and all the time.

Roscoe stuck a microphone in Johnny's face. "How does it feel to find a fellow countryman in such a small town?"

"It makes me feel a little less homesick, mate. It's like having a rellie here," said Johnny, keeping the same plastered smile. How do you like your runners, Nikki?"

"Super!" I smiled.

"Maybe we'll get a coldie after this. Where're you from?" Johnny asked.

"Melbourne," I replied. I've used up my entire Australian repertoire. Why wasn't Roscoe asking Johnny any questions?

"Oy, that's where I was born. I have hundreds of relatives that live there. What's your last name?"

I looked at my watch. "Crikey! Look at the time. I need to pick up my five kids from kindie. Need to run. So nice to meet you." I shook Johnny's hand and briskly walked away. I was too afraid to look back. I was sure Johnny knew that I was a fake. As soon as left the club, I made a run for my car. Darn! Why did I have to park on a side street? I heard someone running after me. I ran faster. Just as I was about to reach my car, I felt myself being tackled to the ground.

I screamed. "Get off of me!" It was Alex.

"Funny, you used to beg me to get on you."

He ripped off my wig and took off my glasses. And, then he kissed me. It was a deep passionate kiss and it totally threw me off guard.

"Charlie, what are you doing?" he asked.

"What are you doing? One minute you're trying to handcuff me and bring me to jail and then the next minute you're...."

He pulled out his handcuffs, "...trying to handcuff you and bring you to jail."

"Alex, you can't. I'm getting closer in finding out who poisoned the soup. I have a few suspects that are real possibilities. I think the poisonings are tied to drug counterfeiting."

"Drug counterfeiting? How did you find that out?"

"I can't tell you now. But, if I were in jail, I never would have been able to make that connection. Please, just give me another week."

He looked at me, unsure of what to do. I knew he still had strong feelings for me, but was it enough for him to disregard his job.

"Are you in love with Chad?"

I didn't say anything. I could see this really upset Alex.

"You have one week, and then I have to bring you in. You know, I'm such an idiot for letting you go. If my boss finds out, I'll definitely be fired."

He fell silent for a few seconds.

"Charlie, do you think you could give us another chance?"

"Alex, you have a girlfriend."

"I have someone I live with. There's no love anymore. If I knew you still cared about me..."

"Charlie?"

It was Chad. Alex was still lying on top of me.

"She has one week, and then I'm bringing her in," Alex said to Chad. His demeanor had totally changed. "If there are any real leads, though, I need to know about it. This is still my jurisdiction. And, I will be following you."

"Counterfeiting is my jurisdiction, mate," said Chad.

"One week, Charlie," said Alex. He slowly lifted himself off of me and walked away.

When Alex was out of sight, Chad said, "Let's go back to my place. I can't wait to look at the naked picture of Andi."

"Excuse me?" I asked incredulously.

"For professional purposes, of course," Chad said. "Let's go back to may place. Demo Day is done."

As we slid into my car, big raindrops started to paint the windshield. I loved the rain. It gave me a feeling of comfort and protection.

This time when I showered at Chad's, I was pain free. I held onto him tightly as the water firmly ran down our bodies. I could feel all my tension being released.

"I need to tell you something, Charlie," said Chad.

"I don't like the way you said that."

"I need to fly back to Paris this weekend."

"Are you coming back?"

"I, I don't know."

"Is it work?"

"Not exactly."

"Sabine?" I suddenly let go of him. I just knew.

"Blimey, you're good. Sabine and I need to talk about a few things."

"Hello, haven't you heard of a fabulous discovery called the video chat, or the cell phone, or…"

"I need to talk to her about you. And, I can't very well do that here."

"So, you're going to fly all the way to Paris? Is she your girlfriend? Did you tell her about me?"

He quieted me with a kiss and a few other things.

"Hey, did they teach those moves in spy school?" I smiled.

"We have work to do," he said seriously.

He gently nudged me out of the shower.

"I'm getting pressure from my boss, Sabine, to make more progress on the counterfeiting connection here."

"Sabine is your boss? "

"The drugs are being manufactured in Puerto Rico, then shipped to various countries in Asia. Sabine is thinking of relocating me to Puerto Rico."

"Oh, she's good. She's really good. She just wants you as far away from me as she can get you."

Chad responded to me by making us tea. I quickly learned it was the British answer to breaking bad news gently.

We sat on the living room couch in silence as we drank our tea. Finally, he said, "You know, I'm not a perfect person. I have a history of extraordinary shallowness. I'm 42 years old and never been married. I have been proposed to at least 10 times over the years, and I have led too many women on. I have good instinct in my work, but somehow I don't allow myself to follow that instinct in my relationships."

"So, what's your instinct telling you about me?"

"That I think you could be the one had we more time together."

"Had? You're scaring me."

"My job takes me all over the world. You live in Bucks County. Now, let's see that naked picture."

I gave him an incredulous stare. I knew he had reached his serious quotient. And, realized that maybe that was why he was still a bachelor. I presented the infamous picture of Andi Miller and principal Paul.

"Oy, she's a good looking girl," he said.

"There's something else I found in her bag." I pulled out two neatly folded handwritten notes. "They're IOUs. One of them is signed by Eddie and the other one is signed by Henry.

"For how much?" Chad asked.

"Eddie's is $150,000. And, Henry's is $300,00."

"Wow!"

"I know. Boring Bucks County, right? We've got a married principal having an affair with two women, one of them married. We have a hamster that was poisoned with a counterfeit "vitamin" pill, two women poisoned by cyanide in their soup, a manic sports-betting pro and a psychotic tennis stringer in debt to a wealthy, adulterous tennis girl."

"You left something out. Henry used to deal drugs for the pros on the tour. Maybe he's still dealing. It's plausible that he still has overseas connections," said Chad.

"Have you looked in his office?"

"Of course. Unfortunately, the most interesting things I ever found were a bunch of articles about his drug trial. They were crumpled up in his desk drawer. I've also scoured his emails maybe a dozen times and copied the directory on his computer.

"Wow, you're sneaky."

"Sneaky is my job."

We both sat in silence for a bit.

"You know what I think? I think if Andi were dead than neither Henry or Eddie would have to pay her back. Since Henry almost went to jail for counterfeiting drugs, it wouldn't take much for him to still have access."

"So, you think Andi is next?" Chad asked.

"Well, if I were her, I wouldn't be eating any soup in the near future."

"Rough town." Chad gave out a low whistle. "Where do you think Andi got all that money to lend to Eddie and Henry?"

"Her husband is CEO of Tower Glenn. Beaucoup bucks. She's a multi-billionaire. Maybe the thought of being a high-class loan shark was exciting to her. I mean, she's posing naked with a married man. There's obviously another side to Andi that we didn't know about. How many times have you read about people leading double lives? She's a bored billionairess looking for thrills. Hmmm…that's a great headline." I grabbed Chad's laptop and started writing another segment of "Notes."

"Then how do you explain the deaths of Grace and Lilly?" asked Chad.

"Both Henry and Eddie know that when teams play here, it's the AWAY team that eats first. Andi was part of the AWAY team, the Mood Swings. Grace was an unfortunate casualty. I don't think either one of those guys would have cared if they knocked off the whole team. As long as Andi was dead, they wouldn't have to pay her back."

"Okay. That may explain Grace. But, why was Lilly's soup poisoned?" Chad asked, clearly not buying my theory.

I just got a text and thankfully it wasn't Edith. I speed dialed Robin.

"Hi, I miss you," I said.

"I miss you, too. Listen, I just discovered something that I think you'll find quite interesting."

"You found out what Jim Greco actually does?"

"No."

"Roscoe's been fired?"

"No."

"Edith hit on Prudence?"

"No."

"Prudence hit on Edith?"

"Charlie! Just listen. Phil invited me over last night and guess who came to dinner?"

"Sidney Poitier?"

"Charlie, be serious! It was Phil's sister."

"So?"

"Her name's Julie Quinn."

"Crikey!" I put my cell on speakerphone.

"Well, during dinner Julie broke down crying. She said she had been having an affair with a married man and she just ended it. So, we asked her why. She said it was because the man she was having the affair with was also having an affair with her sister, who was also married."

"'Her sister?' What's the sister's name?

"Adrienne. No, wait a minute, it was Andrea.

"What's Andrea's last name?"

"I don't know. It didn't come up. I didn't think to ask."

"Well, the only Andrea I can think of is the one I saw at Bucky's funeral. And, I only saw her from behind."

"The hamster funeral. Right. I'm texting Phil now. I'll find out her last name. But, I'm not sure how that's going to help you."

"Did you find out anything else?"

"One other thing...one other big thing. Phil's garage was open when I pulled into his driveway. So, I decided to walk into the house through the garage. On a shelf I notice a bunch of chemicals. At first I didn't think anything of it because Phil is an exterminator. But, I did decide to take a closer look. One of the containers was labeled cyanide, Charlie. It gave me the heebie jeebies just looking at it."

Chad and I stared at each other in disbelief. Phil? Just as I thought we were beginning to piece the puzzle together it had begun to fall apart.

"Did you mention the cyanide to Phil?"

"No, I didn't want him to think I was accusing him. Maybe it's normal for exterminators to keep cyanide in their garage."

"And just because he's storing it in his garage, doesn't make him guilty, but it is suspicious." Chad said.

"Well, let's think about this. He had access, the means, but what was his motive?" I asked.

"I know Phil had exterminated the club the day Grace was poisoned. I remember the club was infested with cockroaches and they had called an exterminator," Chad said.

"I actually remember an exterminating truck parked in the lot as I was running into the club. Who could forget that huge cockroach painted on it and that stupid slogan: "You got'em…Phil kills'em"?

"Could I be dating a murderer?" Robin sounded horrified.

"He does sell the type of oils that were slipped into Lilly's soup, he did exterminate the restaurant where the poisoning happened, and he did exterminate Mill Creek the morning of the murder," Chad said.

"Could he just be a crazy person and didn't need a motive?" I asked.

"Great. I'm dating a sadistic psychotic," Robin said. She was sounding more frantic by the second.

"Well, they don't call them 'exterminators' for nothing!" I couldn't help adding.

"Charlie! I'm having a nervous breakdown. Stop!"

"Is all cyanide created equal? That's the question. If not, we need a sampling of Phil's cyanide and match it against the cyanide found in Charlie's bag and both the soups."

"That's a good point," Robin said. "I'm googling as we speak," she said. We waited a few seconds. "It is. It's just the strength of the cyanide that could set it apart when used. But, that doesn't matter. Cyanide is cyanide. 'Birnbaum.' Phil just texted me back with Andrea's last name."

"Andrea Birnbaum? That's Bucky's mother!" I said. "So, all three siblings had access to the Cyanide: Phil, Julie and Andrea."

We heard a loud buzz.

"Ugh, I'm being summoned by Edith," Robin said. "I've got to go. Keep in touch."

Chad and I looked at each other.

"We know that Julie was in possession of a counterfeit drug. But, we still don't know who fed the drug to the hamster. And, maybe it wasn't an accident that Bucky was fed that drug."

"Are you implying it was Julie? But, why would she want to kill a hamster on purpose? That's too weird and random. Makes no sense," I said.

"Doesn't it? We now know that Andrea, Julie's own sister, was having an affair with her boyfriend."

"Her married boyfriend."

Chad was pacing. I felt so bad for him. He was clearly frustrated.

"I've been here for almost a year and this is all I've got? It's embarrassing."

I took a look at all the racquets Chad had stacked in the corner of the living room. "I'd better give Andi back her tennis bag tomorrow. I bet she is beside herself that she's lost it."

"Especially because those I.O.U.s were in there," Chad said.

"Yeah." I picked up a few of the racquets and took some swings. I picked up a Prince and could barely get my fingers around the grip. "This can't be a 4 3/8."

"It's not. It's a 5 ½."

"5 ½! Whose racquet is this…Godzilla's?"

"Close. It's Grace's," Chad said nonchalantly. "Well, it was Grace's."

"Grace's?! What the ding-dong are you doing with Grace's racquet? Why were you holding out on me? Did the police see this?"

"Did you just say, 'What the ding-dong?'"

"Yeah. So?"

"What the hell is that?"

"Where I live, sometimes kids will ring your doorbell and run away. My kids call it a 'ding-dong ditch.' Don't they have that in England?"

"Oh, yeah, we have that. But we call it, 'If you ring my bloody doorbell again and run away, I'm going to beat you to a bloody pulp, until your insides are sprawled out all over the bloody street.'"

I cleared my throat. "That must be the, uh, special Euro edition of that game."

"And, by the way, I am the police. I'm entitled to this evidence."

"You know what I mean. Alex and Oversized. Did they get prints off the racquet?"

"Yeah. They fingerprinted it, they analyzed the paint, but I wanted to see it. I had a talk with Alex after I saw him on top of you. I went to the police station the next day. I asked to see Grace's racquet, figuring the police probably took it. And then I told him…" Chad said, pulling me into his arms. "If you tackle my girlfriend again, I'm going to beat you to a bloody pulp, until your insides are sprawled out all over the bloody street."

I laughed. "You didn't. Did I hear you say girlfriend?"

"Much to my office's chagrin, you are one of the reasons I'm still here. Like I told you, they want to relocate me to Puerto Rico. We need to find the manufacturing plants producing the counterfeit drugs. I keep stalling, saying that I'm on to something here."

I picked up Grace's racquet and handed it to Chad. "There's no way a human could hold this racquet comfortably. Even if Grace was a big girl."

Chad lifted the racquet, and stared at the grip. "Hang on, there is something peculiar with this grip."

He began to unpeel it and saw there was another grip under the one he just peeled. He unpeeled the second grip. We both got excited. But, there was nothing underneath the grips but wood. He banged the butt of the racquet against the floor in frustration. Suddenly, the piece that's in the middle of the butt of the racquet popped out. He looked at the inside. Something was pushed in there. He went to a drawer and pulled out a zippered kit. He picked up tiny tweezers. After a few seconds, he pulled out a thumb drive. We were stunned to say the least.

"What the ding-dong?" is all Chad could say.

"Crikey," I answered back.

He pushed the thumb drive into the back of his computer.

We saw a series of bank statements.

"There are several transfers from a Swiss bank to her local bank here. Why did she go to the trouble of putting these statements on a thumb drive and then hiding it in the butt of her racquet?" Chad asked.

"Every girl knows the safest place to keep her jewelry is on herself. Grace was a lawyer, she knew the importance of key evidence," I replied.

"Hadn't she ever heard of a safe deposit box?" asked Chad.

"Are you going to share this information with Alex?" I asked.

"Bloody, hell no," Chad said. He dialed his home office. "Sabine...

CHAPTER 16

I was waiting in Chad's car till the very moment7I had to play. Today was Districts. The day where the top teams in each division battled each other like gladiators in a sweat-filled, pressure-packed arena. Actually, if I had to pit a gladiator against a tennis girl, I would put my money on the tennis girl every time.

The playoffs were being held at Fieldstone Tennis Club in lower Bucks County. The top teams in levels 3.0, 3.5, and 4.0 would be playing today. I looked through the back window and couldn't believe how mobbed the club was. Several teams were sitting on blankets they had spread on the grass. The club had 10 Har-Tru courts and it looked like they were all being used. Of course, as I was self-quarantining myself in the car, my vision was somewhat limited.

As I sat squirming, I decided to write another installment of "Notes." According to Edith, my column now had a cult following. "They want to tweet you, Charlie. Do you think you'll be able to get those tweets from where you are?" Edith had no idea what tweets were and she still had trouble understanding how the Internet worked and didn't trust it. Her office bookshelves were lined with Webster's Encyclopedias from the 70's. I typed Edith back, "Tweets come from me, not the other way 'round."

Suddenly, Savannah popped her head in the window.

"We're on, honey."

"I'm nervous," I said. "What's everyone saying?"

"Well, the big topic of conversation is whether you're going to show up or not. Jazzy and Collette are hoping you don't show so they'll get a forfeit. One of their singles players isn't feeling very well."

"Is it the college girl they had flown in from Florida?"

"No. It's their other singles, Missy Smith."

"Oh, she's really good. She played for a Division 1 school. What's our team saying about me?"

"Devon said she's going to beat you up if you don't show."

"She didn't. She is such a bully."

"Listen, honey, don't worry about her or anyone else. It's just you and me on the court today. If Devon lays a hand on you, I'll punch her in her patooties. Not many people know this, but I was on the men's boxing team in college."

Savannah opened the car door and I gave her a hug.

As we walked towards the courts, I could see everyone staring and whispering. Elaine was at the registration desk. She saw us and exhaled a big sigh.

"Charlie, you showed! I wasn't sure whether you were in jail or not. You need to sign in."

The girls from our team, High Strung, were hanging out under a shade tree by the courts. I knew I shouldn't join them, but I did.

"Can you believe the Mood Swings asked Henry to be here, in case they snap their strings?" said Barb.

"I think it's too late for that," I joked. Everyone laughed and looked relieved to see me.

"We need your court," said Devon seriously.

"You don't plan on winning? " I asked her.

"The Mood Swings have college girls for both singles," said Devon.

"Pressuring me is not going to make me play better, Devon." What a jerk. I turned and walked away. I am so finding a new team next year. That is, if I'm not behind bars.

I suddenly turned around and walked back up to Devon. "You know what? You're a bully. And, I'm sick and tired of you always being so confrontational. Just because you don't have high hopes for your match, doesn't mean you have the right to put pressure on me for mine. I'll play my match, and then I'm done with you and this team.

Everyone was stunned. I had never spoken up for myself before. Elaine ran up to the group and broke the silence.

"You and Savannah are playing on court 7."

"Now?" I asked.

"Now!" said Elaine. "You're playing Jessie and Maria Theresa. Devon, you're on court 2, Maryellen, court 4, Jen and Barb are court 9, and Tracey and Susie are on court 8."

I knew Jessie and Maria Theresa's games inside and out. Maria planted herself on the baseline and tried to set up Jessie, who was quicker than lightening at net. Jessie reminded me of a jack-in-box because she seemed to pop up unexpectedly at net, intercepting balls in split second notice. She definitely had the poaching gene.

I quickly filled Savannah in on the games of both girls. Our game plan was to try and keep everything away from Jessie, and try and keep our balls deep to Maria so she couldn't step into her shots. Also try and chip short to bring Maria in where she wasn't comfortable. The big problem, however, was not going to be our opponents' tennis games, it was going to be Maria's big boobs. I didn't say this to Savannah. I was hoping she had had sex the night before. She had brought her partner, Chelsea, with her. Focus on the balls not the boobs, I would tell her.

As Savannah and I walked to our court, I looked around at all the cliques from the different teams and then I took a deep sigh. The personalities, pressures and politics of the tennis world were wearing me down. More so, than my impending incarceration for crimes I didn't commit. As if reading my thoughts, Savannah rubbed my back.

"How're you doing?"

"Feeling like I'd like to curl into a ball and roll away." I could feel my nerves bouncing around my body like pinballs.

"Remember you're playin' with me, honey. No pressure."

As we were about to walk onto our court we saw Maria Theresa, Dal, and Jessie holding hands in a circle. They were chanting something.

"Well, I'll be derned," said Savannah. "Do you think they're trying to put a hex on us?"

And a second later…

"Well, would you look at Maria's top? Tight and low, just the way I like it."

Her hormones were unbelievable. "Savannah, I'm giving you a mantra for the match: 'I will keep my mind on balls not boobs.' Wait a minute, that didn't come out right. Let me rework your mantra."

"Got the gist, honey. No worries."

Jessie and Maria waited till we walked on to the court. Then after a minute, they casually walked on. It was gamesmanship, making us wait. They were wearing their team colors: yellow and white. Savannah and I forgot to wear our team colors: turquoise and white.

I looked outside the fence and already a crowd was forming. I was notorious now and a curiosity. How would she perform under this pressure?

Maria measured the net as I spun the racquet. Savannah's eyes followed Maria as she squat down to adjust the net and I hit Savannah in the butt with my racquet.

"Remember your mantra," I said to Savannah.

We won the toss and let Jessie and Maria serve first. They chose the side with the wind in their face and the sun at their back. Smart.

"Let's win this for Grace and Lilly," Maria said, loud enough for us to hear. Then she and Jessie did a high five. And, Maria did a quick sign of the cross before they walked to their side.

"Maybe we should do something," said Savannah.

"Yeah, let's win so we can shut them up," I said. "They're looking way too smug."

I always say that the first four games of a set don't count because everyone is not only nervous in the beginning, but you're also feeling out your opponents, learning about their game. No one held serve the first four games, and I attributed that to nerves. The Mood Swings had a huge peanut gallery and they would wildly clap and holler anytime Maria and Jessie would win a point. They would even clap if Savannah and I made a mistake. And, that got me really angry. Savannah and I stuck to our game plan and won the first set 7-5.

We were up in the second set, 3-0, when Jessie hit a swinging volley straight at my head. The other times she had aimed at my head, I managed to duck, but this time I wasn't quite as lucky and fell backward onto the ground. I could feel my eyes rolling to the back of my head and all I could see were cartoon stars.

"What the hell do you think you're doin'?" screamed Savannah to Jessie.

"Watch your language," said Maria.

"We're calling a time out," said Savannah.

"That's fine with us," said Maria.

Savannah pulled me over to the side. She took some ice in the cooler, put it in a towel, and gently placed it over my eye.

"Ow!" I screamed.

"Ah, know. But, I don't want your eye blowin' up. Can you open it?" Savannah took the towel off.

I slowly tried to open it, but it hurt.

I heard Maria and Jessie walk over. "According to the Code, Rule 30, you can't take longer than 90 seconds on a changeover, or 25 seconds between points. I just wanted you guys to know, so you don't get penalized."

Uh, have you heard of the word "chutzpah?" With all my energy I lifted my head.

"Well, according to the code, hitting a ball at a person is a 4-point penalty and you can get disqualified or ejected," I said.

Just then one of the roving umpires walked over to us.

"What's happening here?" the umpire asked

"Charlie got hit with a ball on purpose," said Savannah.

"That's a lie!" snapped Jessie.

"She must have hit four or five swinging volleys at her on purpose. I mean, at this level, you shouldn't be aiming at people's heads," Savannah said.

"Hitting at someone is part of the game," said Maria.

"But, not intentionally at their head," cautioned the umpire. "I'm giving you a warning. The next time, I'm going to disqualify you."

"If you do that, then we're going to report you to the head of the league," said Jessie. "You can't disqualify someone for how they hit the ball. It's subjective."

"I'm giving you a one point penalty. You can't talk to an umpire like that. I'm giving the young lady another minute for an injury time-out."

"That's good. This will break up their rhythm," I heard Maria whisper to Jessie as they walked away.

Savannah pulled me up on the bench, making sure not to press the towel of ice over my eye too hard. When she finally pulled it off she said, "Are you sure you still want to play?"

I heard Elaine at the fence. "Do you think you can still play?"

I turned around, and Elaine gasped. My eye probably looked like something out of a horror movie now. Elaine continued without looking directly at my face. "I don't want to put any pressure on you, but our singles are getting killed. We need all three doubles."

"Time!" The umpire called.

I pushed myself off the bench and pulled my sunglasses from my bag, wishing I had been wearing the glasses before I got hit. I slowly walked to the Ad side.

Maria was about to serve when we heard from the court next to us, "Are you sure? That's the third ball you called out that hit the line."

"The ball was close, but it was out," one of the girls said.

"But your partner called the ball out on the sideline. That's your call. You're closer."

"Excuse, me," I called over to the other court. "Can you keep it down?"

"I want a line judge!" I heard Jen yell from the other court.

The umpire hanging around our court walked over to the other court.

Maria pounded a T-serve when Savannah wasn't ready. Luckily it was just out.

"Out!" I called.

"That was an ace," said Jessie. "I saw it. It hit the T."

"It was on my side of the court. It was out!" I yelled. I had lost all patience with them…and women in general.

"I want a line judge," said Jessie. "That's like the fourth bad call you've had."

What's the date today? Aargh! Mercury is still in retrograde. I decided to blame her screaming at me and hitting me on purpose on the reverse pull of that planet.

Suddenly, there was screaming from another court, the one to the right of us. We were playing on the middle court. We all turned and saw a girl slam a ball at another girl's stomach. Then a ball was slammed right back at her head.

"Bitch!" I heard Jazzy call out on the other court next to us.

"You cheated to win the 1st set, but I'm not going to let you do it the second set. We're not playing another point until we get another line judge. We want two!" Jazzy demanded.

My attention quickly went back to our court.

Savannah and I were in our ready positions waiting for Maria to serve. But, Maria was walking in a semi-circle. She would begin serving when she was ready. Aka: gamesmanship. But, Savannah had had enough.

Savannah, who towered over all of us, walked up to net and said to Maria and Jessie, "Ya'll gonna quit stallin' or are ya'll gonna play?"

Jessie took her racquet over the net and pushed Savannah in the stomach. "Who do you think you are trying to push us around?"

Savannah pushed Jessie back in her stomach with her racquet. I saw Maria massage her cross, and sign herself. She didn't know what to do. I could see a mid-life melee in the making. And, it was a deadly hormonal cocktail: angry, peri-menopausal women mixed with the craziness of mercury in retrograde. But, looking over at Maria Theresa, still rubbing her cross, I knew whose side the mother, son and the Holy Ghost were on. We were clearly outnumbered.

Savannah and Jessie, meanwhile, were in full battle mode. They were actually swinging at each other with their racquets. Swing Boxing, new sport. The girls from the other courts had stopped playing and walked over to our court to watch.

"I was a boxing champ at my college, Missy," said Savannah, bobbing and weaving around Jessie.

"Oooh, I'm scared. Do you see me shaking?" said Jessie, whacking Savannah on her back.

Boy, we really were like gladiators, multiple gladiators. My eye was really bothering me now and I was seeing double and triple of Savannah and Jessie.

A few of the pros and the District coordinator ran onto our court trying to break up the boxing match which was getting more intense. They futilely tried to get the matches on either side of us to keep playing. There were many teams waiting for these courts to finish so they could go on.

Suddenly, I heard police sirens. "Shit!" I quickly packed up my stuff and ran as fast as I could towards Chad's car. There was still an APB out on me. Even though Alex had graciously given me one more week to work on clearing myself, I was sure these cops wouldn't be as kind. I ran off the court.

"Charlie, where are you going?" screamed Elaine. "You can't leave. We'll have to forfeit. We need your court to win!"

"She's a fucking felon," I heard Jessie scream back. "Even if you won, you'd have to forfeit anyway. A felon's not allowed to play. She would have been DQ'd."

These women were psychotic, all of them.

I didn't stop running until I reached Chad's car. Thankfully, the extra set of car keys was still clinging underneath the front tire. I pulled them off, beeped the front door open, keyed in to the ignition and hastily weaved my way down the windy driveway of the club. Unfortunately, I was still having a hard time seeing, and almost hit a group of tennis picnickers on my right. I think I must haven driven over the edge of their blanket because they all got up and started screaming at me. Then they started throwing fruit at the car. Oranges and bananas hit the rear windshield, and somehow, an errant apple made its way through a small opening by my window and hit me on the head.

Man, were we a scary tribe or what?.

CHAPTER 17

I drove directly to Jitters. Nothing like a cup of coffee to calm
your nerves. I threw on a wig and glasses and walked into the
coffee shop. I was drowning my sorrows in a triple mocha
Frappacino when I got a chilling text: "Go to jail, go directly to
jail or your next destination will be your children's burial site.
Camp food can be deadly."

I stopped breathing. I immediately called camp and told
them that until my husband or I could pick up our kids, they
were not to drink anything that wasn't from an unopened bottle
or eat anything that wasn't from an unopened can. I immediately
forwarded the text to Marshall and Chad.

I dialed Marshall's cell. "Did you get my text? Can you get
the kids now?"

"If anything happens to the kids, Charlie, it's all your fault.
You're running around in disguises like it's a game. You're a
fucking fugitive, for God sake. Turn yourself in already. Let the
cops handle this."

"They have no suspects but me, Marshall. We live in a small
town and the cops need to solve this to make them look good.
I'm going to talk to a few people today. I think I know who did
it."

"Who?"

"I'm not going to say." Because I'm lying, that's why. "Just go get the kids! Okay? If I get them, then it will turn into a circus."

"Alright. I'm going now."

Whew! What a relief. At least my kids would be safe with Marshall. I didn't want to go to the after Districts party. But, now the murderer was drawing my kids into it. What type of person would threaten innocent children?

Jazzy's party was going to be huge. The party was being held outside her house under a tent. She had hired a DJ, and it was being catered. I asked Robin to come and bring Phil. She didn't want to come, but I begged her. I needed to question everyone, one last time. There would be so many people that nobody would question why he or Robin were there. The Mill Creek staff and all the travel teams were invited. Okay, maybe the majority of people wouldn't be talking to each other, but it would be maybe my last chance to question possible suspects. I was also tired of running from the cops. So, if I were caught, so be it. And, then I would need a high-powered, celebrity lawyer to get me off. Isn't that where this whole thing started; me worrying if I could afford a good lawyer?

Just then, Chad walked through the door and sat down next to me.

"Who knows your kids are at camp?" Chad asked.

"Of my tennis 'friends'? No one, really. The only person who knows they went to camp this summer is Robin. Wait a minute, Phil not only knows they went to camp, but he knows what camp they're at. I mentioned it when the four of us went out together. He said he went to the same overnight camp when he was younger and then he became a counselor there. But, we still haven't figured out his motive."

We sat in silence, deep in thought.

"Maybe Eddie or Henry stole cyanide from Phil's truck when he was exterminating the club, earlier that morning, before the match. Eddie saw an opportunity to kill off Andi, or maybe Henry stole the cyanide to help out Nora by poisoning the soup and damaging the club's reputation."

"Let's not lose sight of the fact that Julie somehow got access to a counterfeit drug. I believe that she fed it to Bucky on purpose. Remember the principal saying he couldn't see her doing any heavy lifting? I think she made up the story she told you. Could she have some connection with Grace who was getting bi-monthly deposits of cash from a Swiss bank?"

My mind was going round in circles.

"We're talking a double murder here. Who do we know that has no conscience?" Chad wondered.

I gave him a look that said who don't we know that has no conscience.

Just then, Funky walked in to Jitters wearing a t-shirt that said, "Funky Can Fix it!"

"Oh no." I buried my head in hands. But, it was too late. Of all the coffee houses, he had to walk into mine.

"Hi, Charlie. I towed your car back to my shop. You left it in a deserted lot. Why'd you do that?"

"Well, why did you leave naked pictures of Julie Quinn in my glove compartment?"

"Oh, that was an accident. She's a nice looking women, ain't she?" He gave his toothless whistle. "But, her sister's even nicer lookin'. I got some polaroids of her, too."

"Andrea Birnbaum?" I asked.

"No, Andi Miller. At least that's what her insurance card said when I inspected her car. Man, she's got some headlights on her." Funky laughed at his own tasteless joke.

"Andrea was Andi?" I tried to give a whistle just like Funky's. Only, I still had my front teeth, so I couldn't replicate his sound exactly.

"How do you know they're sisters?" Chad asked.

"Andi said her sister was picking her up when she had to leave her car to be inspected."

"How'd you get the naked pictures? You know what, on second thought, I don't want to know," I said.

"You'd be surprised the things people leave in their car, especially their glove compartments."

Thankfully, he walked over to the coffee counter to place his order. We watched him get his coffee but then he walked back over to our table.

"Can I join you?"

"I'm sorry, Funky, Chad and I need to talk right now."

"That's okay. I'm a good listener. Remember how you used to tell me all your problems?"

"Funky, that was in 12th grade, over 25 years ago. Listen, I think you're a nice guy, but Chad and I need to be alone."

"Oh, I get it. I'm not good enough…because I'm a mechanic." He gave me a disgusted look.

"No, I like you, but, my kids, my life, everything is very complicated now. I need to sort things out. You actually helped me out a lot with this case."

"You still wanted by the cops? That disguise ain't no help. I knew it was you when I walked in."

"I'm not good at being on the lam, I know."

"Good luck, Charlie. I won't turn you in."

Funky gave me a defeated toothless smile and walked out the door. The words "I do it with wrenches" were plastered on the back of his shirt.

"So Chad, Andrea Birnbaum is Andi Miller. That means Andi had access to the cyanide and was there at both poisonings."

"But, so was her brother," Chad said.

"Well, that settles it. It was either Andi, Phil, Nora, Henry, Eddie, the whole Mood Swings team, my team, or anyone else who ever played ladies tennis."

I took a deep breath. "So, when are you leaving for Paris or Puerto Rico?"

"I'm actually going to Switzerland now. I'm meeting Sabine at the bank that issued the transactions to Grace. I was set to leave tonight, but…"

"Tonight? It's all Sabine's fault. She doesn't want you near me."

I blew the froth of my mochacinno in Chad's face.

"Hey!"

My cell phone buzzed. Savannah texted me: "our match DQ'd bcoz u r felon. Mood swings won 3-2. Team is REALLY mad at u!" I showed Chad the text.

"They put you in the line-up. They knew your situation."

"Can I come to Switzerland, too?"

"You have kids that need you."

"I know. They're the only thing that's keeping me halfway sane. I've decided I'm going to Jazzy's tonight and just confront everyone. I have nothing to lose. I'm going to jail anyway."

"Don't say that. You do have a lawyer by now, right?"

"Not yet. I don't have the money."

"Charlie!"

"I guess I better get my stuff together at your place and move back home. Till they come and get me that is."

"The police?"

"No the tennis girls. They'll come in a mob...at night...hundreds of them, charging the house, armed with pitchforks, and torchlights. Do you remember the mob scene in 'Frankenstein?'"

"Charlie!"

CHAPTER 18

I did my best thinking in the shower. And, as I let the hot water pour down over my head, I decided that if I were going to go down tonight, I would go down in style. I was going to look good, dammit, and no more playing the victim. I had lots of good leads and suspects. The murderer had to be someone who was both at the tennis match where the first poisoning happened and who was also at Sacre Bleu! that night.

Of course, Phil was still a prime suspect. He had exterminated the restaurant and was in the kitchen and so was Henry who was doing the dishes. And, of course there were all the people sitting at Plug's table. But, you would think she would have noticed if someone at the table slipped something in her soup. So, maybe it was Phil. And, just like that, I became defeated again. It could be one of 10 people! Not counting Eddie who was at both places also.

I toweled off, blew out and flat-ironed my hair. I pulled out my magnifying mirror, and began the process of putting on make-up. I put on my black, skinny jeans, a cute, white, sleeveless top, grabbed a black jeans jacket, and stepped into my peep toe black booties.

I took a look at myself in the hallway mirror. I looked good, really good. Be confident, I said to myself. And, be alert. The one person, besides Savannah, who had my back was already on his way to Switzerland.

"Now it's too late baby, now, it's too late..." Carole, I hope you're wrong. I picked up my cell phone, thinking that I meant to change my ring tone weeks ago. I looked at the number. It was Alex.

"Alex?"

"I figure my butt's already in trouble for letting you go a few days ago, so I thought why not give you a heads up that a squad car is being sent to your house to pick you up. There's another APB out on you."

"I thought there already was a APB."

"It's a Federal APB. The feds have gotten involved, Charlie. They want to make the murders a federal crime, because the penalties are much tougher. It would be a feather in the Governor's cap to have this murder solved. I guess you haven't been listening to the news lately, but Gilbosky decided yesterday to run again. He's behind 10 points. Capturing you would prove that he's not soft on crime."

"Well, I guess someone has time to listen to the news."

"It's on in the station 24/7. I can also tell you that there's an 80% chance of rain tonight."

"I'm going to Jazzy's party tonight. I have a few people I want to talk to (uh, like 10), if I don't find out who did it, then I'll turn myself in after the party. But, I need you to promise me that you won't tell the cops I'm at the party."

"If I called to warn you about the cops, then I think you can trust me not to turn you in...tonight. You have my promise. By, the way, I broke up with my girlfriend. And, before you can say anything, it's not because of you. It's because I don't love her and repeat, it has nothing to do with you. Well, maybe a little. I do have a soft spot for cute, Australian tennis players."

"Ausie, Ausie, Ausie oy, oy, oy," I chanted sadly. "Wish me luck."

"I wish you luck."

I drove to Jazzy's. I was about an hour late and the party was packed. I circled twice around the block, but there wasn't one space available. I finally parked illegally next to a fire hydrant about 20 feet from Jazzy's driveway. What the heck, in comparison to all the other laws I was breaking….

I slowly (my peep-toe booties, setting the pace) made my way up the hill to Jazzy's palatial home. Catering trucks were parked on her circular driveway. I saw a huge tent that had been set up behind her house. Loud music was blaring. I heard the end of Gloria Gaynor's "I Will Survive" and then "Burning, Burning, Disco Inferno." She had hired a DJ, who was doing a tired 70's set.

I decided not to go through the front door. I didn't want to make a splashy entrance. My bravado had diminished a bit, and I found myself unhinging the gate that led to the side door of the walkout basement.

I walked in the basement, and was thankful the light was off. I knew where the door was that led to the wine cellar. I hadn't brought anything to the party, except the opportunity to turn myself in, that is. I still thought it would be pretty funny to bring Jazzy a bottle of her own wine. I opened the wine cellar door and began futzing around for the light, but couldn't find it.

No matter. I had my trusty tennis racquet flashlight that dangled from my key chain. I turned the little handle and a small stream of light guided me towards the racks of wine. I read some of names and quite a few sounded familiar. Being a food critic, I had sampled quite a few of these wines. I settled on a very expensive Chateau Mouton-Rothchild. I saw another bottle of Chateau Rothchild that was dated 1945. I gave my best Funky whistle. That bottle probably cost at least $100,000. Where do these people get this kind of money?

I was about to turn around when a box labeled "Tennis Balls" caught my eye. Hmm. If someone could afford racks and racks of pricey wine, they surely wouldn't miss a few cans of balls. I was conveniently carrying my cute Kate Spade tote bag. Perfect for stowing almost anything. I could probably fit one can of balls and one bottle of wine. If I was going to jail, I might as well go out in style. I didn't care if I was caught with the goods.

I peeled off the packing tape of the large box and pulled out a can of balls. Out of habit, I pulled off the green plastic top, to make sure the balls were new and sealed. When I opened the lid, I didn't see the round tin seal that all new ball cans have. I took out a ball, and it looked new. But, there was a weird sound inside of it. I shook the ball. What was that noise?

Just then, the lights went on. I let out a scream. I tried to hide behind the big box, but couldn't fit my whole body.

"Charlie?"

I recognized the voice and let out a sigh of relief.

"Jazzy sent me down to get a few bottles of her really pricey wine; to celebrate their victory."

"Please don't tell Jazzy I was hiding in her wine cellar, and that I stole a bottle of one her best wines, and took a can of her tennis balls. I was still clutching the wine I was going to give to Jazzy.

"What are you doing in here? Nobody even thought you'd come to the party."

"Because everyone is mad at me?"

"That and because your face has been plastered across all the local news shows. Everyone wants you, Charlie. And, no one wants you more than me."

"You? What are you talking about?"

"Do you have a minute? Of course you have a minute. But, that's probably all you have."

"Cindee, you're acting really weird. What are you talking about?"

"I see you opened that box of tennis balls," Cindee said.

"How do you know that I opened them?"

"Charlie, you're a nice girl, but a bad liar."

"That's where you're wrong. I happen to be a great liar," I tried to joke.

"Shut up, Charlie! Just shut up! I need to do what I have to do, finish the trifecta, and then I'll be free. Debt paid."

Trifecta? Cindee's the one who killed Grace and Lilly? I started grabbing around in my bag for my cell and pulled it out.

"Cindee, listen, I need to go. It was a bad idea to come to the party. I'll see you at the club."

Cindee kicked me in the shins and then pushed me down.

"Cindee! What is your problem?"

Suddenly, I heard a lot of voices, and then the lights went off in the cellar. My heart started beating so fast I thought it was going to bounce right out of my body.

"Did you do it yet?" It sounded like Devon.

Eight flashlights turned on, illuminating eight familiar faces: the Mood Swings team. Minus Grace and Lilly, of course.

"Jazzy, I'm so sorry about going in your wine cellar," I said.

"You mean, breaking into my wine cellar and stealing two really expensive wines. Each bottle has been catalogued and has its own electric alarm," Jazzy said.

"Actually, I was only going to steal one bottle, I mean, take one. The other bottle I was going to give to you. And, I'm really, really sorry."

"You were going to give me a bottle of one of my own wines? You, know, I was sort of feeling a little sorry that you had to be killed. But, now, not so much," Jazzy sneered.

"I'm going to be killed for stealing your wine?"

"Stop playing dumb, Charlie," Andi said.

I was playing dumb, trying to bide time. Thinking how I was going to escape being poisoned by these nine lunatics. That's how they were going to do it, the same way they killed Grace and Lilly, with poison...Phil's cyanide, to be precise. My cell was still balled in hand. I kept speed dialing Alex and Chad, hoping I was hitting the right numbers of course. But, if Sal's pizza came to my rescue, I wouldn't care. I didn't even know if I was getting a connection in the cellar. The sad truth was that Chad almost certainly couldn't help because he was probably still on a plane. And, how would he interpret my constant calling him? How would he or Alex know that I needed help ASAP? Why did I tell Alex to promise me he wouldn't let the cops know I went to the party?

I pulled out the can of balls from my purse. I shook a ball.

"What's in here?"

"Drugs," said Collette. "Counterfeit Alli."

"What are you doing? Don't tell her," Maria Theresa said, nervously rubbing her cross.

Andi grabbed the ball and sliced it open with a small kitchen knife she was holding. She pulled out a few small bottles of pills. "Our warehouse in Puerto Rico produces the pills, then they ship them to us, bottled. We cleverly package the bottles in tennis balls and send the boxes to our "camp" in Malawi. The "camp" office, or S.C.A.M, as we cleverly called it, was our little joke with the initials: Serving Children of Africa's Malawi."

"S.C.A.M? More like S.C.U.M!" I said. "Taking advantage of people's generosity."

I received another smack in the face from Cindee for my retort.

"Ow!" I could feel my face burn.

"Who are you to be so Goddamned righteous? You always have to have a sarcastic comment about everything, don't you?" Cindee sneered.

Andi continued. "Anyway, the S.C.A.M office paid us by wiring us money from another location, to a Swiss Bank.

"No name on the account so it's not traceable," Jessie said.

"Smart. But, why kill Grace and Plug?" I asked.

"Grace was the team treasurer," said Andi. "She was a tax attorney, so it made sense for her to be the point person of the account. When Grace decided that both she and Plug wanted out of the operation, they both had to be killed. They knew too much."

"So you tried to kill both when you poisoned the soup at the tennis match. But, how did you know they would be the first one's to eat it?" I asked.

"We were the Away team," Jazzy said. "The Away team always eats first. And we knew Grace and Lilly were chowhounds. Wherever we played our matches, they were always the first ones to eat. So, we came up with the idea to poison the soup and let them eat first. And, if anyone from your team died also, well, that would just be a bonus."

"Yeah, kill Grace, Lilly and eliminate your team from Districts all in a matter of minutes. Brilliant, I must say," Jessie smiled.

The girls laughed at this. I truly believed that decades of competitive tennis had made them this heinous and numb to any empathy.

"Cindee, how did you get involved?"

"What do you care? You'll be dead in a few minutes. You would've already been dead if you didn't have such a big mouth! Andi, why don't you cut out her tongue? That'll shut her up."

I couldn't believe how psychotic Cindee had become. She was deranged.

Collette, who was a bundle of nerves, kept tying and untying her scarf. "No, zay all must die zah same way, by poison. Zere must be no blood on zah team's hands."

"I don't see any harm in telling Charlie, she won't be leaving this room," Andi said. "Cindee had a huge credit card debt, so she asked Eddie to place some bets for her. Well, she lost all her money on the bets. And then she couldn't afford to pay back the Mafia, who wanted the interest paid to them, like in 2 days, for placing the actual bets for Eddie. Cindee was in a panic, so she came to me, knowing I had lent money to Eddie and Henry."

"Why didn't she come to you in the first place, before she went to Eddie?" I asked.

"I was embarrassed," Cindee said.

Andi continued. "So, I told Cindee I would pay the Mafia debt for her, if she would be the executioner for us. All she needed to do was slip some cyanide, provided courtesy of my brother, into the soup you made and the soup at the restaurant, and for good measure slip some cyanide vials into your purse. We wanted to pin the murders on someone who was under a lot of stress, so the murders would seem more plausible.

"And, Lord knows no one seems more stressed than you," Devon said. "In fact, you look a little stressed right now," she smiled.

You are such a jerk, Devon. Why do people like you, and all of you, always get away with everything?

"Hey, Maria, what would God think about you killing me and poisoning people with dangerous drugs?" I asked, hoping to make her feel guilty enough to stop another murder.

Cindee smacked me. "Shut up! Charlie! You have a big mouth. You've always had a big mouth...acting so smug and thinking you're so smart."

Tears started rolling down my cheeks. I couldn't help it. I didn't want to give them the satisfaction of seeing me cry. My only hope was trying to make them turn on each other. Make them question killing me. I remembered seeing a window in cellar, but I didn't know if I could reach it, or find it. The only light in the cellar came from The Mood Swings' flashlights.

"She's right. How can I justify these killings?" Maria asked.

"Because you're not the one doing the killing. It's Cindee," said Jessie.

"You're all accessories to the crime. You're all equally guilty if you ever get caught...when you get caught," I said.

"We are? But, we didn't murder Grace and Lilly, Cindee did. It can't be equal." Maria was a bundle of nerves.

I could barely make out Cindee taking a capsule from her pocket.

"Enough, talk, let me just do this and then I'm done!"

"I have one more question," I said. "Who took the oil from my desk and poured it into the soup at the restaurant?"

Cindee responded. "I poured the oil into Plug's soup, but I didn't take it from your desk."

"I stole the oils from my brother's store," Andi said.

"As luck would have it, I happened to see Robin in Phil's store, buying a candle and a vial of oil for you. That's when I decided to take some oils. I had thought when the analysis of the soup was done, it would just point the finger more in your direction. I never thought it would get Phil in trouble, or I never would have done it. You know, if it wasn't for Phil, I don't think we, I mean Cindee, could have pulled off the two murders."

"What about the poisonous mushrooms?" I asked.

"I also took them from my brother's store. I told Cindee to slip them in the soup you made. Just in case the cyanide didn't

167

work. I thought adding the poisonous mushrooms would be a nice touch to the soup. A little texture never hurt anyone. Oh, yeah...I guess it did!"

Everyone laughed again.

"But, you all have a lot of money. Why deal with counterfeit drugs?"

"Because you can make billions of dollars, and there's a huge market for them. That's why," said Ginger.

"Haven't you been reading your own paper, Charlie? For the past several years, there's been a huge downsizing in pharma companies, CEOs being fired left and right. We're all used to a certain lifestyle. We became tired of wondering whether our husbands were going to keep their jobs every year. When Jessie's husband, a senior VP at Tower Glenn got laid off three years go, we knew we had to do something drastic to make money," Jazzy said.

"But, wait...." I said, trying to continue my talkathon.

And as my mouth formed the "w", Cindee stuck the capsule in my mouth. I bit down hard on her finger and spit out the drug.

"Ow! You bitch!" screamed Cindee.

I ran as fast as I could, trying not to bump into the racks of wine. I even threw some bottles at the girls as they ran after me. Glass and wine splattered everywhere. I pulled a bottle of wine from my totebag. "Jazzy, I'm holding a 1787 Chateau Lafitte. I swear I'll throw it on the floor if you don't let me go."

"Shit!" yelled, Jazzy. "That's a $114,614 bottle of wine that Eric and I just won at an auction. Girls, we have to let her go."

"What, are you insane?" Cindee said. "Then, she'll go right to the cops and we're all screwed."

"She's right," Andi said. "Fuck your bottle of wine. Let's get her!"

I threw down the pricey bottle and its precious contents scattered onto the floor.

"Charlie, what you just did was blasphemous. Have you no culture? Get that bitch!" Jazzy screamed.

"Ow, ow, I'm stepping on glass. I think I got cut. I'm bleeding," Devon cried.

I managed to get to the door of the cellar and felt my hair being pulled back.

"I've got her, I've got her!" Andi said.

"Ow!" I screamed. I gave a backward soccer kick and hit Andi's shins. Thankfully, she loosened the grip on my hair. I quickly opened the door and made a mad dash outside. I could hear the girls running behind me, cursing at me. Luckily, I was a fast runner, and fear made me faster. I quickly ripped off my booties and flew to my car.

I grabbed the magnetic key on the front wheel, and just made it into the car, just as the girls caught up to me. I started the ignition. They lined up in front of the car. But, at this point, I didn't care if I mowed them over. I lurched the car forward and the girls parted like the red sea. I drove directly to the police station, because that was the safest place to be. I would take jail time over these psychotic tennis Looney Tunes any day of the week. It would be nine against one when we told our stories to the cops. But, I was tired of running and I would take my chances.

When I arrived at the station, I parked in the lot and took a deep breath. I looked at my cell. Neither Chad or Alex had tried to reach me. I pulled down my visor and looked in the mirror. My face was covered with cuts and bruises from Cindee slapping me. I broke down and cried.

After a good ten-minute cry, I walked into the station and saw Alex pacing at the front desk. I gave him a weak smile.

We walked into an empty office.

"The next time I tell you not to let the cops know where I am....don't listen to me," I said. "I guess you didn't get any of my calls. I kept speed dialing your number. Actually, I was hoping it was your number. I was in a wine cellar."

"No, I spent the last few hours pacing around the station. Wondering what was happening to you. Your face says it all. You poor thing."

We hugged each other. I hadn't felt safe in such a long time.

CHAPTER 19

I placed two new 8x10 pictures of my boys on my new desk in my new office. I looked at the Delaware River from my oversized window, and couldn't wait to go tubing with my sons. It was a corny ritual and we went every summer.

Robin poked her head in.

"So much for the protection candle you gave me," I joked.

"I know. I'm sorry," Robin said.

"I still don't know who took the oil from my desk, though."

We gave each other a big hug. Today was my first day back at the Bugle after my ordeal. Thankfully, the DA had no trouble convicting Cindee of the two murders, and the other eight girls were accessories to the murders. Because of the convictions, the Mood Swings were DQ'd at Districts and my team, High Strung, was declared the winner. We now were scheduled to play sectionals in August. And, if we won that, then we traveled to Arizona for Nationals. I began daydreaming of me riding a horse along a scenic path at sunset. Hot diggity-dog, I hope we made it to Nationals!

"Hey!" Bradley gingerly walked in. He gave me a little soft shoe.

"You're all better!" I bent down and gave him a big hug.

Suddenly, we heard the dreaded Edith buzzer. "Meeting in the conference room in 10 minutes…"

"Let's play hooky," I whispered.

"...I heard that. I won't tolerate tardiness from anyone...even you, Charlie," Edith said via intercom.

"Damn! She's good," I said.

"Hey, did you ever find out about the autopsy and why Bucky was poisoned?" Bradley asked.

"I did call the vet hospital and an autopsy was done. Bucky did eat a Peanut Chew, and it was poisoned. It was laced with cyanide, courtesy of Julie Quinn, Andi Miller's sister. Julie and Andrea Birnbaum, aka, Andi Miller, were unknowingly having an affair with the same man, a married principal. Julie killed her sister's hamster with the poisoned peanut chew as retribution, when she found out about her sister's affair. She also took a few of the counterfeit pills from one of the tennis balls her sister had stashed at the house. Julie found out about the counterfeiting and was hoping to get Andi in trouble without her going directly to the cops. She dropped a few Alli capsules in the classroom, hoping that would lead back to Andi." I was proud I was able to regurgitate the whole sordid story.

"Talk about your sinister sisters," Bradley said.

Prudence pranced in carrying a bottle of champagne and stack of paper cups. She poured us all a cup. "When it rains it pours. I have a confession to make, Charlie."

We all became silent. "Prudence, please don't tell me that you were in cahoots with those horrible tennis girls," I said.

"I was the one who took the vial of oil from your desk."

"You?"

"I mean, why should you be the only one to get protection? I needed protection also. I was afraid that Edith was going to find out that I was auditioning for the YNOT job. So, I snatched your oil and bought a candle at "Kibbutz and Kabbalah" the same color as yours," Prudence said.

Prudence refilled my paper cup. "Drink up! It actually tastes better after the 4th cup." Prudence let out a big belch.

"Prudence, there's a meeting in....now!" I gasped.

We all looked at our watches. Uh, oh. We all became quiet. We heard the familiar click clack of Edith's wooden heels down the hall. Suddenly, she burst through the door.

"Charlie, I should have known you were behind this…this unsightly coffee klatch. That's why I asked this young man to make sure he keeps our resident ring leader on time from now on." Edith actually smiled.

Chad walked in! I thought I was going to faint.

"Cheers, everyone!" Chad said in his native accent.

"I thought you had moved to Switzerland. You're staying?" I asked.

"I needed to stay around so I could tie up a few loose ends," he smiled.

"Promises, promises," I smiled back. Yikes, did I just say that? I felt myself blushing. There I go again, blurting out inappropriate things. Thankfully, Roscoe burst in, breaking up the awkward moment.

"The conference room was empty. Why didn't anyone tell me there was a party in here?" Roscoe was huffing and puffing.

There was an awkward silence.

"I have a toast to make. 'To 'Volumes from the Underground.' I have a lot of material," I sighed.

Everyone stood up and clinked their champagne cups. "To 'Volumes.'"

Edith looked intrigued. "Volumes? I like it. 'A recap of the madcap.'" She made a large gesture with her hands, like she was reading it on a billboard. Her eyes began to glaze. "We'll do installments. Keep them hanging. They'll be paying us double before I'm through… aching to learn the real underpinnings of the tennis world." She pulled out her plastic cigarette holder and hit my desk with each tennis plague: "poisonings, Mafia, sports betting, counterfeiting, the occult, double murder."

I thought Edith would faint she was so excited. I found myself unable to get this stupid Cheshire smile off my face. I never thought the sound of Edith's voice would make me so happy.

THE END

CHARLIE'S FAVORITE RECIPES

CHEATER'S CHILI

2 tablespoons vegetable oil
1 pound diced, cooked chicken meat
1 onion chopped
2 cloves garlic, minced
1 (14.5 ounce) can chicken broth
1 jar tomatillo salsa
1 (18.75) can of tomatillos, drained and chopped
1 (16 ounce) can diced tomatoes
1 (7 ounce) can diced green chilies
½ teaspoon dried oregano
½ teaspoon ground coriander seed
¼ teaspoon ground cumin
1 (15 ounce) can white beans
1 large bag frozen white corn
1 bunch fresh cilantro, chopped
Salt and ground black pepper

Directions:
Heat oil, and cook onion and garlic until soft.
Stir in broth, tomatillos, tomatoes, chilies, and spices.
Bring to a boil then simmer for 10 minutes.
Add corn, chicken, and beans; simmer 5 minutes. Add chopped cilantro at the end of cooking. Salt and pepper to taste.
Serve with grated cheddar cheese and tortilla chips.
Serves 8-10

ON THE LAM YAMS

5 large yams or sweet potatoes
3 tablespoons of butter
¼ cup of orange juice
¼ cup of milk
Salt and pepper to taste
1 bag of Marshmallows (optional)

Directions:
Peel potatoes and cut into small cubes.
Place in a large pot and cover with water.
Cover and bring to a boil.
Cook about 20 minutes, or until potatoes are tender when pricked with a fork.
Drain off water. Mash with a potato masher.
Add butter…keep mashing…add orange juice, milk and salt and pepper to taste…mashing all the while. Whisk potatoes a bit with a wire whisk until nice and smooth.
If topping with marshmallows, pour potatoes in a 9X13 inch baking dish. Top with marshmallows and place under broiler until brown….for just a few seconds!

LYING LIME BARS

2 ½ cups all-purpose flour, divided
½ cup sifted powder sugar
¾ cup butter
½ teaspoon baking powder
4 large eggs, lightly beaten
2 cups sugar
½ teaspoon grated lime rind
1/3 cup fresh lime juice
Powdered sugar

Directions:
Combine 2 cups flour and ½ cup powdered sugar; cut in butter with a pastry blender until crumbly. Spoon mixture into a greased 13X9 inch baking pan; press firmly and evenly into pan, using fingertips. Bake at 350 degrees for 20-25 minutes or until crust is lightly browned.
Combine remaining ½ cup flour and baking powder; set aside. Combine eggs, 2 cups sugar, lime rind, and lime juice; stir in flour mixture. Pour over prepared crust.
Bake at 350 degrees for 25 minutes or until lightly browned and set. Cool on a wire rack. Dust lightly with powdered sugar; cut into bars.

ABOUT THE AUTHOR

Ever since being inspired by Nancy Drew at the age of 10, Gigi Arnold has been writing mysteries. She was a Communications major at American University, and played on her college tennis team where she was MVP her freshman and sophomore year and captain her junior year. She studied at NYU graduate film school, moved to LA, wrote several screenplays (mysteries, of course), and has also authored 24 children's mysteries for the Sneaker Seekers mail mystery series. She currently resides in Bucks County, PA, plays on several competitive women's league tennis teams, including USTA which continues to provide a never-ending source of material.

9175460R0

Made in the USA
Charleston, SC
17 August 2011